Betty McEachern

Through Cast Iron Gates

Published by:

FriesenPress

Suite 300 – 852 Fort Street

Victoria, BC, Canada V8W 1H8

www.friesenpress.com

Distributed to the trade by The Ingram Book Company

CHAPTER ONE

Aubry MacNicholl was born to parents Grace and Francis in Halifax in the summer of 1893. She was a beautiful baby, having inherited the best of her mother and the best of her father. From her mother, she had inherited her crystal blue eyes and warm and inviting smile. From her father, she had inherited her red hair and prominent nose. It was not long before her 13th birthday that she started to flourish.

By the time she was 17, she had become the object of affection of many smitten and foolish men. Her long red hair, which she usually parted to one side or the other, ended at the small of her back with a whisper of a wave. Her smile was captivating and held a hint of playfulness and a hint of shyness, which she used to her advantage in social situations.

She was so stunning men would take notice from across a crowded room and be driven to try to make a connection with her. Oftentimes, these same men would long to be in her company well after her scent had faded. Even married men would let fantasies play out that would bring them to their knees in their darkest hours, leaving them nothing more than infidels. Aubry knew she was stunning; she knew she had the ability to leave even the strongest-willed men weak and ruined.

Yet there was a part if herself she kept hidden very well, like a secret kept between best friends, never to be revealed. She knew she was different. Though embarrassing as she might have thought her certain personality traits to be, and as much as she kept her heart under lock and key, she knew that one day, in order to be loved and in order to love as deeply as her heart desired, she would have to reveal herself. Truth be told, sometimes her passions and desires overwhelmed and even frightened her. For her, each day was a blessing, and she spent much of her time day dreaming and longing to be fulfilled.

What she dreamt of most often was love that most people would never be able to conceive of, a love so powerful and engaging; it would be all-consuming. It would more than exist; it would flourish through any storm life would bring. She wanted a man who was as passionate as she was, a man who was strong, so strong that he could surrender himself to her entirely. Many dreaming days and sleepless nights this desire had taken hold of her and refused to let go.

Until she was 23, the fates would not allow Aubry to be loved this way. At 23, with her future ahead of her and her teaching degree in hand, Aubry went to work at St. Joseph's Grade School on Kaye Street. It was a brisk 45-minute walk from her house at 16 Inglis Street, where she still lived with her parents.

St. Joseph's was an all-girl Catholic school that included students from grades 1 to 8. Aubry, being one of only three teachers not to be a nun, had often butted heads with some of the sisters, who not only thought Aubry did not belong, but also saw her as a temptress. Aubry was aware of the disapproval and the scorn that followed her down dark and empty corridors. Still, she had her pride and she enjoyed teaching.

Her first year of teaching, in 1916, was a test of her dedication. Her 7th grade class consisted of 38 girls, many showing promise and an aptitude for literature and history. At the top of her class were three girls, Anne, Marie and Jane, and they were always competing with each other to see who could obtain the highest grade on the latest math test, or who was chosen to read out loud a passage from the Bible. On occasion, other students would share in their classroom notoriety. It brought Aubry great joy to teach such capable and attentive students.

It seemed that the children sensed the tension between the sisters and Aubry, and played this to their advantage. One cold autumn day there was an incident that would call into question Aubry's ability to maintain control over her classroom. With her back to the class, she looked out towards Halifax Harbour and slipped into one of her daydreams. She imagined herself wearing the most beautiful, sinful red dress. It exposed her bosom and ran just past her knees. Her arms were exposed entirely from her shoulders down. Her lover and husband held her in his arms and kissed her so deeply that she felt she would melt. He spun her around and they began dancing. Their embrace was…

"Miss MacNicholl, Miss MacNicholl!" As suddenly as she had found herself in the arms of her lover and husband, she was back in her classroom, and in the garbage can next to her desk burned a small fire.

"Children, stay calm and form a line single file toward the classroom door," she ordered. The children obeyed. Two children at the back of the line were giggling and pointing. "Diane and Louise, this is no time to," she began but just then the flames climbed the legs of her wooden desk and assignments, books and supplies caught fire. "Children, please move quickly to the main door and gather outside by the playground."

"Miss MacNicholl, what's that burning smell?" Sister Mary inquired, running from her classroom. In seeing the flames, Sister Mary, nearly yelling, said, "Goodness, we must get the children out of here and notify the fire department." Ten minutes later, all 398 children were present and accounted for. Eight minutes after that, horses' hooves falling heavily on the narrow road announced the arrival of the fire department.

By the time the flames were extinguished, the classroom had been badly damaged. It had be gutted and cleaned extensively before Aubry's class could return. The work took a week and a half and during that time, Aubry had to share a classroom with Sister Mary. It became apparent to Aubry that Sister Mary regarded her with scorn and disdain, and the students knew that Aubry might be teaching with borrowed time, as well as with borrowed books.

Aubry was called before the headmistress, and an explanation was demanded. Aubry did not know for sure how the fire had started or who had started it, so she could offer little in the way of answers. Indeed she was *told* she was teaching on borrowed time. If another such incident occurred this school year, and with such consequences, Aubry would have to look for work elsewhere. After all, someone could have been hurt, or worse. Teachers needed to be in control in their classrooms, and students needed to know that teachers were to be respected and rules were to be abided by or there would be consequences.

Christmas break neared without another incident. It seemed as though Aubry and her class had developed a mutual respect, and the children had become drawn to her. She had a way with her students that the nuns did not. Oftentimes she would take her students on class trips to further engage them. History lessons were often taught at the armouries, students visited the Richmond Printing Company to see where newspapers and the like were printed, and the Acadia Sugar Refinery in Richmond to see where sugar was refined and produced.

On the last day of class before Christmas break, a low pressure system formed out in the Atlantic Ocean and stalled over Halifax. The blizzard brought nearly 30 centimetres of snow to the city, and classes were let out just after lunch.

Aubry said her goodbyes to her students and set out for home. Walking down Campbell Road, with a great wind coming up from the harbour, Aubry kept her head down, her steps were heavy and her breathing was hard. Battling through the storm meant that her walk home would more than likely take the rest of the afternoon, and she wanted to be home in time to cook supper for her parents. Suddenly slipping on ice just outside of Café Halifax, Aubry twisted her ankle and went sprawling. Hitting the ground hard, she was sure she had broken her ankle. With sharp pains starting in her left ankle and running up her left side, she struggled to get up.

That's when their eyes met, and Aubry's heart skipped several beats. Oh, how handsome he was. Curly blond hair framed the most beautiful face she had ever seen. Although in her dreams, her lover and husband did not have defined features, surely this magnificent, blue-eyed man must be him. His gaze never left hers. His smile was something she would take with her in the weeks that followed.

"Are you alright, miss? Can you stand?" Patrick Putnam inquired. Aubry accepted the gloved hand extended to her and attempted to get up without putting any weight on her left ankle. Patrick, sensing she needed help, grabbed her by the waist and pulled her close to him. At nearly six and a half feet, Patrick seemed commanding to Aubry, who stood only five feet five inches tall. Her body was tingling from his touch, and she let herself be guided by him.

"Thank you, sir. My name is Aubry MacNicholl. I am-more than thankful for your assistance."

"Not at all miss, I am always at the service of a damsel in distress," Patrick offered with a wink. "Please, call me Patrick. Can I offer you a ride, Miss Aubry MacNicholl?" Aubry let her eyes meet his again, perhaps for a little too long, and she was helpless to look away.

"Miss? My carriage is right over there," he said pointing across the street. Leaning into Patrick for support, Aubry allowed herself to be led to the carriage. Surely she would not make it home in this weather, and with her ankle being so sore. Though the pain was nearly unbearable, it still was not enough to distract Aubry, and she allowed herself to be caught up in the moment. She wondered where this nearly perfect stranger had come from and how she could have been so blessed. "Where would you like me to take you?" Patrick inquired, looking into her eyes and never letting his gaze falter.

In the next moment, Aubry felt a rush of excitement as she envisioned their first embrace and their first passionate kiss.

"Miss?" Patrick was smiling quite warmly, increasing Aubry's pulse twofold.

Feeling a little embarrassed for allowing this stranger to see her without the composure that years of schooling had perfected, Aubry managed to speak. "Please, 16 Inglis Street will be splendid."

CHAPTER TWO

On a number of occasions after her fateful meeting with Patrick, Aubry frequented the Café Halifax, hoping to see him again. She could not erase the image of his smile, or the feeling of safety he gave her. She truly felt he was her destiny and she would not be happy with any other man.

On one such day in January, Aubry arrived at the café just 20 minutes after school had let out. She saw what she thought was Patrick's carriage just outside. With her heart beating faster than it ever had before, she entered the restaurant. There he stood, by the counter speaking to a ravishing beauty, who Aubry overheard Patrick call Francine. Aubry thought her worst fears were about to be realized. She had not allowed herself to think that this mysterious stranger, the one she could not get out of her mind, could be married.

Aubry had turned to leave when Francine called out, "Miss, can I assist you?" Aubry froze. Patrick turned around and his eyes met Aubry's. "Aubry, it is wonderful to see you again. I trust that your ankle is feeling better?"

Aubry broke her gaze and looked at the floor. "Quite, thank you again for your help."

"Good, then would you like to take a walk with me?" Aubry nodded, her voice temporarily lost.

"Splendid. Let me get my coat." Three minutes later, Aubry and Patrick set out on a cool January afternoon, walking south on Campbell Road. Neither of them spoke for several blocks.

"Halifax is beautiful in the winter, isn't she?" Patrick inquired. "Citadel Hill sits in her majestic glory, in the middle of a grand port town, bearing down on the wonderful city of Halifax. She truly is a grand protector. There is an abundance of trees and a harbour that is so fit to accommodate for industry and pleasure. Halifax is bustling, and I am overjoyed to be one of its benefactors. Do you know that I own the café, a hotel and a movie theatre?"

Aubry was stunned. Surely Patrick's attire suggested wealth, but Aubry was taken aback. "So, Café Halifax is yours?" Aubry was surprised at how confident she sounded now.

Patrick nodded in agreement. A silence fell upon them for only a few moments.

"Your wife must be very pleased," Aubry said.

Patrick laughed a deep, throaty laugh. "I am not married. If you are referring to Francine, she has been in my employ since the café opened. It was in 1911, and Café Halifax was my first venture, with money from my father's estate, God rest his soul."

"My condolences," Aubry offered, hoping she had not exposed a wound.

"Not at all," Patrick reassured her. "My father, Thomas was a shrewd businessman and a steady provider. I have always wanted to follow in his footsteps. Here I am at the age of 28, an established businessman who wants for nothing. I truly am blessed."

Aubry smiled. "Please tell me about yourself, Aubry," Patrick inquired.

"I am 23, I teach Grade 7 and I live with my parents. I am an only child. My childhood was wonderful. I feel that I have led a life of privilege, and at times even extravagance." Aubry paused.

"Go on," Patrick urged, sensing a change had come over her. Aubry hesitated. She smiled at Patrick and let the silence linger. She thought she might reveal herself to this magnificent man because she certainly felt at ease in his company. But she hesitated and the moment was lost. This time, the silence stretched on as they neared the end of Campbell Road and turned onto Inglis Street. Sensing their time together was drawing to a close, their footsteps slowed.

Suddenly Patrick stopped. He turned to Aubry, and she stopped too. He reached for her hand and pulled it close to him as he spoke.

"Meet me this evening, at the Town Clock at 6 p.m. Say that you will."

Aubry's head was spinning and she closed her eyes for one magical moment. "I will meet you this evening," she responded.

"Excellent, I will see you at 6 o'clock, and please anticipate a wonderful dining experience." With that, Patrick let go of her hand and they walked the rest of the way to Aubry's house in silence.

At precisely 6 o'clock, Patrick was standing at the foot of the Town Clock, which was an impressive three-story structure that sat at the bottom of Citadel Hill, facing Brunswick Street. The base of the clock was a whitewashed clapboard rectangular structure. The next story was built with a splendid rounded construction so that the clock would sit unobtrusively on top of it. The clock bore Roman numerals and was four-sided so the time could be seen from all directions.

Patrick held in his hand an exquisite gold locket with 01/02/1917 AM engraved on the back. He had just come from the M.J. Jewelry store on Campbell Road. He carefully placed the locket back in the red velveteen box that bore the store's imprint and placed the box in the pocket of his overcoat. In anticipation of his meeting with Aubry, his heart beat unsteadily, and his throat was dry. He swallowed hard.

Holding on to the railing at the top of the steps, he looked towards the beautiful harbour below. There were many vessels docked in the harbour, some wartime supply ships on a temporary stay in Halifax Harbour, some cargo supply ships, and some pleasure craft. Many could not be seen from his vantage point because they were anchored in the Bedford Basin.

Suddenly, seductively, he could sense and smell that he was no longer alone. Turning around, he looked into her eyes. "You look simply divine this evening, Aubry."

A playful smile spread across her face. Her red lips parted as she spoke. "It is wonderful to see you again, Patrick."

He reached out for her gloved hand, and together they made their way to the clock. Patrick led her inside, and they climbed a flight of stairs. Before them, there was an intimate round room, which was surprisingly warm. The room was illuminated with what must have been 20 candles.

"This is absolutely beautiful, Patrick. I didn't realize there was a room under the clock. How did you do all of this? This is just too much," Aubry exclaimed.

"Sit, Aubry," Patrick insisted as he pulled her chair out.

"Ever the gentleman," she smiled coyly at him. He took his chair and placed it close to hers.

"Would you care for some white wine, beautiful?" Patrick inquired.

"Oh, yes, thank you," Aubry said.

Patrick poured her a glass, and then himself one. "I propose a toast to new beginnings, and a perfect evening with a perfect woman." Aubry brushed her hair back from her face, and their wine glasses clinked.

Finishing their first glass of wine in silence, and becoming more and more lost in each other's eyes with each sip, the two were interrupted when a woman with black hair tied back in a bun approached. "Sir, your meal is to be served now," Patrick's employee announced.

Following that, three young ladies appeared, one with serving dishes, and two wheeling a stainless steel cart. Upon the table they placed pineapple baked ham, steamed carrots, broccoli, honey-glazed pears and baked almonds.

"Would you join me in another glass of wine, Aubry?" Patrick asked as he poured a second glass of wine. About halfway through her second glass of wine, Aubry could feel her cheeks flush. Patrick leaned in closer.

"You are absolutely the most stunning woman a man could set his eyes upon. You are mysterious, hauntingly beautiful and endlessly quick-witted. I endeavour to get to know you better, Aubry MacNicholl." Patrick could feel his heart quicken, his palms were a touch sweaty and his head was spinning. He was completely enthralled.

"And I, you." Aubry offered, simply. They ate the rest of their meal in silence and solitude.

"Let us walk," Patrick offered. "It is a lovely evening." Hand in hand, they left the Town Clock behind them and walked down Duke Street, towards the harbour.

Since the First World War had begun, in 1914, only minimal lighting was permitted so that the city would not be distinguishable from the sea. In the darkness, Aubry could tell they were nearing the harbor with its familiar aromas of salt air, fish and seaweed. Turning right, they walked along in silence. When they reached the waterfront, they stopped. A cool breeze came in off the water, causing Aubry to shiver. She stole a glance out into the Halifax Harbour. It was utterly dark, and nothing was distinguishable. How eerie it looked at night, Aubry thought.

Patrick pulled Aubry closer to him. Facing her and lifting her chin up towards his face, he kissed her gently on the lips. When he pulled away, he caught a glimpse of her smiling, semi-parted lips under the soft glow of one of only three lights permitted to illuminate the waterfront. This time, it was his turn to shudder and not because of the breeze coming off the harbour, but from the all-consuming desire he felt for her.

The lovers stole a few moments in each other's eyes, each feeling a mutual hot rush of desire in unknown territory, each searching the other's eyes for some unknown reassurance, each holding their breath as if it were their last, so that they might die in that moment where time stood still. They were unable to feel anything else but their untainted passion.

Two people passing by, one drunker than the other, stumbled into the couple, breaking their perfect moment. Without a word, Patrick took Aubry's hand and turned her in the direction in which they had come. When they had reached the foot of Duke Street, Patrick reached into his pocket and pulled out the velveteen box. Under a harbour light, he presented it to Aubry.

"This is for you, Beautiful," Patrick announced with a smile. Aubry took the box from Patrick and immediately recognized the initials on it. She opened the box, lifted the lid and laid eyes on the most exquisite gold locket she had ever seen. She turned it over and saw the inscription 01/02/1917 AM.

"Oh, Patrick, it's wonderful. Do help me to put it on." She held the locket towards him. He took the locket in his hands and released the clasp. Aubry turned around to face the harbour and pulled her hair to one side. Patrick placed the locket around her neck and secured the clasp.

Patrick spun Aubry around and pulled her close. This time, their kiss was not nearly as tentative and gentle. Instead, it was hard and passionate. Aubry could feel herself getting lost, her body tingled, and their purpose was more intense. Patrick pulled Aubry close to him, close enough that she could feel his manhood grow harder. It excited her more and more, and she slipped her hand down his chest towards the crotch of his trousers. Patrick moaned.

Suddenly, Patrick's carriage stopped beside them. He pulled back, and in the darkness of the night, he grabbed her hand and pulled her up and into the carriage. The driver pulled away, taking them back into the direction of the Town Clock. As they rode on, neither was aware of the life and laughter in the streets, or even where they were headed; they were aware of only one thing, they were about to discover each other. The only thing that existed was their panting and their kissing and their wild hands exploring one another. Patrick slid his hand under Aubry's overcoat and could feel her hard nipples through her dress. Aubry slid her hand down the front of Patrick's trousers and could feel a throbbing between his legs.

At last the driver cleared his throat. They had reached their destination. Grinning, Billy ran a hand across his unshaven face, knowing that his boss would not notice tonight. At six feet four inches tall, Billy was a scrawny man. Uneasy around women, he could scarcely remember a single relationship in his 29 years. He chuckled to himself at how easy it was for Patrick.

"Lucky little shit," he mused. Of course it helped with the ladies that Patrick was a man of means. But something told Billy that this one was different. He could sense it in the way Patrick's eyes took on a whole new light when he spoke of Aubry.

CHAPTER THREE

A few days later, Patrick took Aubry to his movie theatre, Putnam Cinemas, on Campbell Road. He had arranged to have the cinema all to themselves. The silent film *A Fool There Was* was showing, starring Patrick's favourite movie actress, Theda Bara.

When Patrick's carriage arrived outside Aubry's home on Inglis Street, Aubry said a farewell to her parents and joined Patrick in the carriage. By this time, Patrick was so enamored with Aubry he was constantly consumed by thoughts of her. The slightest touch and he was hers. He reached for her gloved hand and held it close to his heart. He leaned in closer to her and kissed her on the cheek.

"You are beautiful, as always, Aubry."

She blushed and brushed her lips against his. She hated to admit that he held power over her. She knew he could see it, and it pained her so, but she was in love. She felt safe with him and trusted him to never hurt her.

The lovers travelled the rest of the way to the cinema in silence. Their eyes never left each other. Patrick never let go of Aubry's hand. She frequently felt as though he were not looking at her, but into her soul. She felt exposed and that was alright because he accepted her for who she was. In turn, Patrick was alive when he was with Aubry; she was vibrant and exciting and unpredictable. She was sexy, and he could see the way other men looked at her and still he knew he was all she wanted. He would protect her and go to any lengths to hold on to her.

When they pulled up in front of Putnam Cinemas, Patrick climbed out of the carriage and reached up and held a hand out to Billy. Aubry was not certain, but it looked as though the pair exchanged something. But she was too distracted by Patrick's buttocks to much care. She thought he had the tightest, most perfect behind. She was suddenly behind Patrick and she reached out to squeeze it. Patrick laughed and turned to face her. "Let's go, beautiful," he shouted happily.

They chose seats about halfway between the screen and the exit. Soon, they were locked in a lover's embrace and caressing each other. Patrick gently turned Aubry's head up towards his and kissed her lightly and deeply on the mouth. He found that Aubry's tongue explored the inside of his mouth. The lovers shared in the longest kiss. Aubry pulled away first and placed her head on his shoulder. The movie was about to start and the lights went down.

Although it was a silent movie, it was clear that Theda Bara was portraying the part of a great seductress whose purpose was to lure successful lawyer John Schuyler away from his family and into her arms. Aubry stared at the screen, open-mouthed. She was astonished to see how closely she resembled Theda Bara. As Bara's lips met Schuyler's for the first time, and he surrendered to her, Aubry's stomach turned. As she noted the similarities between herself and Bara, she thought she might be sick. They both had the same piercing blue eyes and prominent nose. As well, they both had the same high cheek bones and wore their auburn hair about the same length. It was almost as though she were looking in a mirror.

Just as John Schuyler was being seduced by Bara, Patrick turned to Aubry and said, "It's striking, isn't it, how closely you resemble Theda Bara? Yes, the similarities are eerie," and Patrick laughed, his lips brushing Aubry's.

Aubry was stunned. She wondered if Patrick had taken an interest in her because of the resemblance she bore to Theda Bara, or if it was a coincidence, and an unlucky one at that. But, when by the end of the movie, Aubry had seen John Schulyer's family had been destroyed, and his child left heartbroken, she tried to deny to herself that there was any similarity. The lights came on in the cinema. Patrick could see the concern written all over her face and thought he understood. "Perhaps you don't resemble Theda Bara so much with the lights on," he said, attempting to reassure her.

As Patrick and Aubry left the theatre, Patrick wondered if the time was right. They approached the waiting carriage, and Billy shot Patrick a questioning glance, which went unnoticed by Aubry. She was too distracted as thoughts of Patrick's comments about her resemblance to Theda Bara swirled in her head.

Patrick helped Aubry into the carriage and took a seat next to her. "Please take us to the Town Clock," he instructed Billy. Without comment, Billy turned the horses towards Citadel Hill. Aubry didn't speak, and Patrick grew nervous. It was unlike her to be so quiet.

As they approached Citadel Hill, Patrick's hands started to tremble. For the first time in his life, he prepared himself for the possibility that a woman might deny him. He tormented himself by playing out more than one scenario in which Aubry would say no. As his uncertainty grew, he decided it was best to push all doubt aside and speak from his heart.

The carriage came to a stop at the bottom of the steps leading up to the clock. Patrick stepped down from the carriage and helped Aubry. He searched her eyes, which betrayed nothing. He took her hand in his, and they walked up the steps.

Just outside the clock, Patrick stopped and turned toward the harbour. Aubry glanced at him and decided not to break the silence. Together they looked down at the city below, which was for the most part in darkness. It was actually quite peaceful.

It was chilly, and Aubry was getting cold. Despite her overcoat and gloves, the winter's bitter winds whipped through her hair and made her shiver. In seeing that Aubry was cold, Patrick knew the moment had come.

He turned to her and smiled. It was a smile that was just for Aubry, and she knew it. He ran a gloved hand through his curly blond hair, and Aubry's expression softened. She could not stay upset with Patrick, especially when he looked at her that way. It made her feel like she was the only woman in the world, and she tingled. No one else had ever looked at her that way, and she thought no one else ever would.

Still holding Aubry's hand, Patrick fell to one knee. Looking up at her, he had never felt so vulnerable. He searched her eyes in the hopes that he would find the answer to his question before he asked. Instead, he saw surprise and disbelief. His eyes watered, and he began to shake once more.

"Aubry, I kneel before you with my heart and soul exposed. And it is yours and only yours. No other woman could ever measure up to you. I see in you all that is beautiful and wonderful and perfect in this world. And I never want to let you go. I think I have loved you since the day we met. As I have gotten to know you, my love for you has grown stronger and deeper. I have fallen madly in love with you. Will you marry me?"

He looked into Aubry's eyes and he could see that she was full of emotion. He reached into his pocket and pulled out the ring. Aubry removed the glove from her left hand and exclaimed, "Yes, yes. I will marry you. I have never wanted anything more. You are my one great love, and I want to spend the rest of my life with you."

Patrick slipped the ring on Aubry's finger. He rose to his feet and looked down at her. He lifted her chin slightly and lowered his head. Their lips met, and for a few moments the world fell away, and the only thing that existed was the two of them. Patrick pulled away first and threw his arms around her. He held onto her tightly and imagined that he would never let her go.

The chill of the night spoke, and they pulled apart. Patrick could see that Aubry was freezing by this time and gestured to her to follow him. Together they made their way back to the waiting carriage. Billy quickly glanced at Patrick, and he knew she had said yes. He smiled to himself. He had never seen his boss so completely powerless with a woman before.

CHAPTER FOUR

Aubry and Patrick were to be married at St. Mary's Church on Spring Garden Road on July 18, 1917. Father John Forrester officiated the intimate ceremony. There were about 50 people in attendance, which included, on Aubry's side, her mother and father, several aunts and uncles and a few close friends. On Patrick's side, his mother and two brothers, Joseph and Andrew were in attendance, as well as a few close friends, several employees and many business acquaintances.

As Aubry prepared to walk down the aisle, she could feel her father's eyes upon her. Standing in the bride's room to the left of the main church, Francis shut the door.

"Aubry, you look so beautiful. Does Patrick realize what a lucky man he is? Oh how time changes things. Seems like forever and a day when you were small enough that I could carry you to bed at night. Yet, it seems like yesterday when I would see you kneeling beside your bed to say your prayers. Time is an odd way to measure our lives. In the passing of it, sometimes we take comfort and sometimes we do not. Sometimes we feel fear and sadness." Francis' eyes clouded over and his face was twisted in an unfamiliar way. Aubry had never seen such emotion in her father.

"With the passage of time on this day, there is fear, and sadness. No longer can I carry my little girl in my arms or watch her say her prayers by her bed at night."

With that, Francis was taken back to his wedding day, nearly 30 years before. For a brief moment or two, Francis could see Grace in that dress and the resemblance brought fresh emotions welling to the surface, begging permission to break free. Pride took hold of his heart and refused to let go. Aubry could see a change in her father.

"Oh, Father, this is my destiny, and I intend to embrace it with all I have. Patrick and I are meant to be together, to live a long and wonderful life. It is my belief that with the passage of time, you will take comfort in the love and happiness that surrounds you. You have taught me about love, compassion, honesty and integrity. I am eternally grateful to you. You have given me the foundation on which to build my life, and that foundation will be stronger than was ever needed. Thank you for the life you have given me." Francis and Aubry shared an embrace that was suddenly accompanied by music.

It was time for Aubry to walk down the aisle and toward her destiny. With each step she took towards Patrick, she was a step further away from one life and a step closer to another. She closed her eyes for a brief moment, and her world spun in darkness before her. Excitement took hold, and when she opened her eyes and took her last step toward Patrick, and her father let go of her hand, she knew she was home.

Only hearing words, as if listening from some distant place and only speaking words as if spoken by some distant person, Aubry was in one of her daydreams. When Father John said, "You may kiss the bride," Aubry was brought back to the reality of Patrick's warm and quivering lips on hers. It was as if they were kissing for the first time; no one else existed for her, and she explored his lips tentatively at first, and then with much passion.

As they parted and turned toward the witnesses, Aubry gazed upon the faces of young and old, unfamiliar and familiar, family and friends. This was it, this was her time, their time really. As she walked back down the aisle, arm in arm with her husband, Aubry could not recall a time when she felt more at peace, or more sure of her future. At 3:01 p.m., on July 18, 1917, Aubry signed her name for the first time as Aubry Marie Putnam.

Their carriage made its way up Spring Garden Road. Aubry and Patrick sat close to each other, holding hands. With temperatures reaching 30 Celsius, and the sun shining in the late day sky, Aubry thought the afternoon was simply perfect. Only a slight breeze could be felt. Coming to a stop just next to the Public Gardens, Patrick dismounted from the carriage and reached for Aubry's hand. The couple walked through the gates of the Public Gardens and approached the small gathering.

Aubry's mother and father walked on the left of her, and Patrick and his mother and brothers walked on the right of her. Following the walking paths and veering to the right, the newly married couple broke away from their families to have their picture taken atop a small white bridge. In one photo, Patrick was holding Aubry in his arms, and the sun was casting a partial shadow on Patrick's face. When the photo was developed later, the close shot with the shadow across Patrick's face made it look like he was only half there.

They walked through the rest of the gardens, and they took photos beside various flowers in full bloom, next to the pond and beside the grand fountain, which provided wonderful pictures and cherished memories. Aubry would later look at the photos time and again, but always she would come back to the photo of Patrick looking like he was only half there, and she would shudder body and soul.

CHAPTER FIVE

On August 29, 1917, Aubry celebrated her 24th birthday, and Patrick presented her with an unexpected gift. He had moved out of his mother's house, and they had been living with Aubry's parents on Inglis Street since their wedding the month before. Aubry was upstairs, dressing in a most revealing black dress. Although the sleeves, which were trimmed in lace, ran the full length of her arm, the dress was cut low between her breasts and exposed her cleavage. The dress stopped above the knee, a length that Aubry had tailored herself. At 9 in the morning, Patrick was in the kitchen of Aubry's parents' house, drinking his second cup of black coffee. There came a knock at the door. Right on time, Patrick thought and smiled to himself. He called for Aubry to come down the stairs. When she did, he informed her that they were going for a carriage ride.

As the couple seated themselves in the carriage, Patrick instructed Billy to "take the ride slow." He asked Aubry to close her eyes. As the carriage left Aubry's house behind, she could not have prepared herself for her destination. The carriage made its way up Inglis Street and turned right onto Longard Street then left, onto South Street.

Aubry could feel the carriage slow down, and then come to a stop. "Open your eyes, beautiful," Patrick said.

When Aubry opened her eyes, she saw a massive Victorian-style house. The beige three-story home had a charming cobblestone walk leading to the front porch. The driveway was gated with a plaque that bore the name Putnam. All of the windows were shuttered, four bedroom windows, and one living room window in the front, one kitchen, one sitting room, one study, and one bathroom window in the back. White trim detailed every corner; every detail of the house spoke of an elegance that only the truly wealthy could afford.

Aubry was astonished and excited. Patrick could not take his eyes away from her beautiful face. As always, his heart raced when he looked into her eyes. "Shall we go inside?" he inquired as he stepped down from the carriage and extended his hand to Aubry. Taking his hand, Aubry was giddy with anticipation. As they walked along the cobblestone path, their hands entwined, Patrick could not help but feel his manhood thicken a little.

When they reached the front door, they were greeted by Lily, one of Patrick's employees. Patrick turned to Aubry and picked her up with ease. She laughed lightheartedly. As her husband carried her across the threshold, and into their new life, nothing could have been more perfectly wonderful.

The elegant style of the outside continued on the inside. Aubry found herself in the living room, which was a grand size, with a stone fireplace on the far wall. The bay window was quite large, which allowed for an abundance of natural light. The ceilings were high, perhaps 14 feet. The walls were a rich taupe in the hallway, and a creamy green in the living room.

After she felt the warmth of the fireplace and danced from room to room, she came upon the study. Books filled two walls. A large and tastefully hand-carved desk was positioned just under the window. Aubry danced over to it and sat down. Leafing through an imaginary book and peering out on an imaginary classroom, Aubry began to speak in a voice that Patrick did not recognize. "Good morning, class. Please turn to page 33 of your books." Closing her eyes, Aubry daydreamed once again.

Her face took on a warm glow, and a smile spread across it that would arouse any man. A hand went to her shoulder, and Aubry opened her eyes. "Patrick, this is all I could have dreamed of and more. But I..." Patrick's lips brushed hers.

"Are you ready to see the bedroom?" he inquired.

Patrick led Aubry to the master bedroom. Stepping inside the room, Aubry saw a dozen illuminated candles. A dark red curtain hung down over the three-paneled window. The room, being at the back of the house, did not capture much sunlight and with the curtains drawn, it would have been quite dark had it not been for the candles. The bed was along the opposite wall from the window. Aubry slipped out of her sinful black dress and started toward the bed.

Coming at her from behind, Patrick stopped Aubry by putting his right arm around her waist. "Don't move," he commanded. He pulled her red hair away and began with small light kisses at the base of her neck. He kissed down over her right shoulder, then her left. His hands reached around and playfully touched her nipples. She could feel his hot breath on the back of her neck as he kissed her there again. She shivered. She could feel his tongue at the small of her back and she shuddered. He licked down past the small of her back, and his tongue found her rectum, lingering for a moment longer and she liked it.

She could feel the hardness of his manhood push up against her buttocks. As he stood up, he turned her around and by the look in her eyes, he knew she wanted him. He lifted her up and carried her to the bed, where he placed her with her legs apart. He kissed her deeply and moaned. "I love you," he whispered hoarsely. His lips left hers, and he parted her legs further. He moved down to her midsection and stopped. His tongue started off slowly at first, and then licked wildly. Aubry screamed his name over and over again. A storm of heat washed over her, and she came down to where he was.

They kissed long and hard, hands running madly over each other's bodies. Aubry pulled away from Patrick and sucked the small of his abdomen, just above his bellybutton. The sweat on his skin tasted slightly sweet. She threw him on the bed and licked his scrotum, and then took him whole into her mouth. Her rhythm was fast, then slow, then fast again, driving Patrick crazy.

She went back to his lips and then in one motion, Patrick was on top of her, riding deep and forceful. His heart was beating so fast and so hard he thought that Aubry could surely feel it. Just as quickly as he had found himself on top of her, he stopped and threw himself next to her. Finding her clitoris, he began touching her. "Don't stop," she demanded. "Faster, faster." Patrick's fingers obeyed. Aubry's cheeks flushed and intense pain arose in the centre of her abdomen. She found herself enjoying another orgasm. This one was more intense than the first and lasted much longer. "I love you, too, Patrick," she panted, trying to catch her breath. Her clitoris was throbbing.

She threw him down on the bed and was on top of him, moving up and down. The springs in the bed played what would become a frequent and familiar song. He could not remember a time when any woman had been so wet. Her wetness and heat and the constant movement of her body against his, with her breasts beating against his chest as she rode upward, made his throbbing almost unbearable. He let it all go in a torrent of sweat and excitement and collapsed. This would become a nightly, and sometimes a daily event for several weeks as Aubry and Patrick fell deeper in love.

CHAPTER SIX

December 6, 1917, dawned as unremarkable as many previous days. The sun rose at 7:35 a.m. in a blue sky that sang a winter's tune. The morning was a cool zero celsius. As in previous days, Halifax was on the move. Nearly 100 ships were anchored in the harbour, including the Belgian relief ship the Imo, and the munitions ship the Mont Blanc. On this ordinary morning, many were pursuing their routine. The misfortune and hell on Earth that the Imo and the Mont Blanc were about to bring to Halifax would be so horrific, no one could have imagined or foreseen it.

At about 7 a.m., Aubry awoke, instinctively aware that she was alone. As was often the case, Patrick had already left to check in on all three of his businesses, Café Halifax, the Halifax Hotel and Putnam Cinemas. Aubry took a bath and went down to the kitchen for some coffee. Lily always had fresh coffee prepared in the morning.

At a little after 8 o'clock, Aubry was sipping coffee at her kitchen table and deep in thought. In just days, she would be leaving her teaching job at St. Joseph's Grade School. It had been a difficult decision to make as teaching was very challenging and certainly rewarding for Aubry. Patrick had been a central motivating factor in reaching her decision. He did not want Aubry to work and felt quite strongly that he should be the one to provide for the two of them. By no means was this a struggle, in fact quite the opposite. Patrick had amassed so much wealth, that they would never have to worry. Now, he wanted to share his wealth, and whatever Aubry wanted, Aubry could have.

She finished her coffee and placed the empty cup on the table. She rose from the table to leave. As she turned, she was startled by Lily's sudden appearance, which caused her to knock her coffee cup to the floor. It broke into large pieces with jagged edges. Some pieces flew a long way, while a few did not. "Damn it," Aubry cursed, mostly to herself. "What a mess."

"Sorry Mrs. Putnam, I did not mean to startle you," Lily apologized.

Lily was probably in her 50s, five feet four inches tall, and she was a good and sturdy woman. She always wore her grey hair pulled back into a severe bun. Ever the serious one, she always wore her white uniform neatly pressed and stain free. Her face spoke of a life of hardship and struggle. If it could tell a story, every line would tell of an abusive marriage, a husband who was always drunk and a child who never got the chance to grow up. Somehow, she was always perfectly pleasant and professional.

"Mr. Putnam wanted me to tell you that he would be at Café Halifax this morning and then at Halifax Hotel in the afternoon."

"Thank you, Lily," Aubry said. She smoothed out her rose printed dress, which stopped just at her ankles, and made her way to the front door. She put on her wool jacket and winter boots and opened the front door. Looking back for a second, she spotted Lily sweeping the broken bits of the cup into the garbage and noticed the housekeeper had cut herself on the jagged pieces. Aubry could not help but be disturbed. Because of her inattention, not only had she made a mess, but also brought pain to another.

Outside her home, the driver was waiting to take Aubry to work. Leaving her residence at 138 South Street, she noted the December chill in the air and shuddered. The carriage, pulled by two sturdy horses, turned off South Street, down Longard Street and onto Inglis Street. Aubry wanted to stop by her parents' house for a minute to invite them for supper. The carriage came to a stop and Aubry dismounted from the carriage with the aid of the driver. "I will just be a few minutes," she told Billy.

Crossing the street, she noted that her parents' home was dark. It looked as if no one was home. She climbed the four steps to the front door and knocked. After 30 seconds or so, she tried the door, and it was locked. Usually, her parents only locked the front door when they went out. She shrugged, thinking, I'll come back after class, and made her way back to the carriage.

It was always a fairly bumpy ride down Inglis Street. At the bottom of the street, the carriage turned left onto Campbell Road. Aubry had instructed Billy to stop by Café Halifax so she could see Patrick for a few minutes and indulge in another cup of coffee and a blueberry muffin. She loved the coffee at the café; it was strong and fresh.

Passing Cogswell Street and nearing North Street, Aubry noted an unusually large number of people headed towards Halifax Harbour. As the carriage got even closer to North Street, Aubry watched as men, women and children rushed down the street. "Please turn down

North Street and proceed to the harbour," Aubry instructed. She was curious now.

Upon arrival at the bottom of North Street, Aubry spoke to Billy. "Stop here, please," she instructed. She stepped down from the carriage and made her way to the pier. Looking out towards the harbour, she saw two ships, one drifting towards Dartmouth and the other towards Halifax. The one drifting towards Halifax was on fire. She could make out part of its name, Blanc.

Aubry saw a smaller ship attempting to put the fire out. The fire department's newly acquired motorized vehicle, named The Patricia sped by. Feeling that the situation was well under control, Aubry knew her coffee and blueberry muffin would have to wait. She made her way through the gawking crowd and back to Billy. "Please take me to St. Joseph's now; I fear I may be late," she instructed as she sat back down in the carriage.

CHAPTER SEVEN

Aubry arrived at school and made her way to her classroom. The school was nearly empty. At 8:59 a.m., Aubry looked at the six students present. "Well, I suppose everyone is watching the ship burn in the harbour," Aubry reasoned as she peered out her window and down towards the harbour. Aubry could see that the ship's fire had spread, and the vessel had drifted even closer to Pier 6.

She turned to her small class and spoke. "We will wait a few more minutes, and then we will get started." A few more minutes passed. One more student, Jenny Johnstone, made her way into the classroom and sat down at her desk. "Take out your history books and turn to page 13. Good morning, Jenny." Aubry addressed Jenny directly, which made her blush with embarrassment.

Aubry turned her back on her class and reached for her history book atop her desk. She could feel the floor vibrate and she lost her grip on her book. It fell to the floor with a loud whack. Aubry was not quite sure what was happening and hesitantly reached down for her book.

A great and forceful wind blew the window out of her classroom and thrust her forward. At the same time, the ground beneath her heaved and newly formed fissures swallowed debris at random. The deafening noise that accompanied this lasted only seconds. If every man, woman, and child in Halifax were called upon to answer for a world at war, and the fiend that was sent to collect opened his monstrous hand and slammed it down upon the city in pure hatred, the damage might have been less.

The roof had been blown off above Aubry's classroom. Confused, disoriented and in utter disbelief, Aubry attempted to stand. Her left leg had gone through the floor and was stuck in some twisted fashion. She moved her leg in one direction, then the other. She twisted and pulled desperately at her leg. Feverishly, she pulled again, and wrenched it free.

She stood up, and realizing that her leg was not broken, she looked around the room. She could see six of her students on the floor, each holding one limb or another. Where was Jenny? Panicked, she called the girl's name. To her right, her toppled over desk moved just a little, and she could see that it had fallen onto the girl.

Carefully, she started to lift the desk from one side. Looking under the desk, she could see that Jenny had suffered a blow to her head and was bleeding just above her right eye. She let go of her desk with her right arm and removed her scarf and offered it to Jenny. She placed it in Jenny's outstretched hand. "Cover your right eye with it," she said in the most soothing voice she could manage. "Can you crawl out?" Jenny, with one hand holding the scarf on her right eye, moved toward Aubry.

Just as Aubry and Jenny had gotten clear of the desk, debris started to rain down on the classroom. Little balls of fire, timber and metal fell from the sky and landed on the desks and the floor and pelted the walls. Aubry felt the urge to move to the basement.

"We have to get out of here now. Children, can you walk?" she asked. Unable to comprehend what had just happened, six children who were sprawled on the floor rose to their feet. One remained sitting, holding her face in her arms. "Janet, can you walk?" Aubry asked. She walked over to the girl and bent down. She tilted Janet's head upward and could see blood oozing from both eyes. "Oh-my-God," Aubry whispered. Janet could not open her blue eyes to see. "I was, I was, watching- out, out. I was looking – the window," Janet shrieked.

At the sight of Janet's eyes, Aubry began to tear up. She started to help the girl to her feet. "It's not safe here. We have to get to the basement. I'll guide you, but you have to walk. Lean into me and hold my arm for support," Aubry told Janet. Janet slowly rose to her feet, repeating, "The explosion, the explosion." Her wailing grew louder. Her sobs were only interrupted when breathing became a necessity. It broke Aubry's heart. "Come now, we'll be all right. Just walk with me to the door."

While Janet sobbed and repeated the words explosion and harbour, Aubry led her and the other six scared and bewildered children down the hall, down the stairs and into the basement. This was not easy as they had to make their way over fallen timber and around gaping holes. Minutes later, the remains of the roof of the classroom they had just come from collapsed, and the room was ablaze.

Aubry and her students had made their way to the basement of the eastern side of the school. Though the basement was dark and damp and completely unpleasant, Aubry needed some time to think. One thing was certain: she needed to get the children out of the school and to the hospital. She decided that they should avoid all downtown streets and should instead walk along Robie Street, toward Camp Hill Hospital.

Climbing out a basement window, Aubry and the children left their school behind. Aubry looked back and saw that the fire that had started so short a time ago had swallowed the school. She turned her back on the school, focused on the journey ahead and shivered. With Aubry guiding Janet, the lonely eight made their way along Robie Street. The walk was slow because Janet seemed unable or unwilling to push forward. Perhaps it was shock, or perhaps it was pain, but whatever it was, it slowed the silent group down.

Slowing the pace even more was the debris scattered throughout the city. The lives of others lay exposed and pieces obstructed their path. Dolls, books, broken dishes and unidentifiable household objects hampered their advance. Some homes were burning, and some had been were destroyed. Aubry was in utter disbelief.

Jenny stumbled and fell to the ground. Tears were streaming down her face as she struggled to stand. Aubry, with Janet holding on to her right hand, helped Jenny get up. When Aubry looked down, she was appalled to see that Jenny had tripped over an arm. The arm was oozing yellow fluid. When she looked at the hand attached to the arm, four aged fingers were curled over the palm, as if holding something tiny. Aubry could tell that the limb had belonged to a man as it was hard and calloused.

Instantly, Aubry was brought out of her daze and back to reality. They had to push forward. She ushered the children onward and away from the severed arm. As the horror of the situation revealed itself in every step they took, Aubry's thoughts turned to Patrick and her parents. A new sense of panic overtook her, and she knew she had to find them and the sooner the better. Aubry turned toward the children. "I want everyone to hold hands." With Aubry in the lead and Janet holding her right hand, the human chain made its way along the last block to Camp Hill Hospital.

Upon arriving at the hospital, Aubry was greeted by the servant of chaos and the master of horror. The servant of chaos; men, women and children were arriving on foot, in carts, by horse-drawn carriages, and by the occasional motorized vehicle. The master of horror; children were screaming, women were sobbing, and men were moaning as they paced the floor. Several bodies lay on the floor, covered in sheets. One child cried in a corner all by herself. She had been badly burned all over her face, arms and neck. If she was with anyone, it was not obvious. To Aubry, she looked helplessly alone and terrified. The burns looked painful, and Aubry winced. To the left, one man was sitting on the floor slumped over and half of his face was gone. He was holding the other half of his face in place with his hands.

A girl in a volunteer's uniform approached Aubry. "Miss, come with me," the girl said. Aubry and the children made their way to the first room on the right. There were two hospital beds side by side on Aubry's left. The occupants were breathing laboriously and moaning. The volunteer, whose name was Helen, spoke. "Those two were brought in a short time ago. They are brother and sister. No one knows where their parents are. They were found wandering in the Richmond District. According to what I am hearing, the Richmond District is almost all gone."

Helen directed most of the children to sit on the floor. She asked that Janet sit on the makeshift table to the right of the room. "I will see if I can find a doctor," Helen said and turned and left.

About 20 minutes later, Dr. Gerald White entered the room. Aubry never let go of Janet's hand as Dr. White examined her.

"What's your name?" Dr. White inquired.

"Janet, sir," came a tiny response.

"Can you see, Janet?" Dr. White asked.

Janet lowered her head. "No, sir. Well, maybe a little bit of a shadow."

"Follow my finger," Dr. White instructed. Janet stared to the left, while Dr. White had moved his finger to the right. "Hmm." Dr. White rubbed the stubble under his chin. "Dr. Drummond will be along shortly." Dr. White turned to Aubry and ushered her away with a nod of his head.

"Are you Janet's mother?" Dr. White asked.

"No, I am her teacher," Aubry replied. "Her mother's name is Catherine Moore. She lives over on Young Street."

"Dr. Drummond will have to examine her; he is an eye surgeon. I think her vision is 100 percent impaired in her left eye. I think she has some vision in her right eye, but it is Dr. Drummond's decision whether she will lose one or both eyes." Dr. White cast a downward glance, and Aubry could see how concerned the doctor was. Then he simply turned and left the room.

Aubry went back to Janet and held her hand. Within a few minutes, although to Aubry, it felt much longer, Dr. Drummond appeared. He examined Janet's left eye and then her right in much the same way Dr. White had done.

Janet began fidgeting and tilted her head towards the ceiling. Aubry forced herself to look closely at Janet's face. Crusted blood and filth covered Janet's cheeks, lips and chin. A fresh trickle of blood emerged from her mouth as the child had just bitten her lower lip. Janet swung her legs back and forth nervously, and Aubry noted her forehead had creased in lines of concern.

Dr. Drummond cleared his throat and with his left leg maneuvered a non-descript metal bucket to his side. It screeched across the floor. Aubry's gaze shifted from Janet's face to the bucket. Horror crept across her face as she assessed its contents. The bucket was just over half full, and Aubry could see eyes of various sizes, shapes and colours partially submerged in a fleshy and gooey substance.

She gasped, looking at Janet, and in one motion that spoke of years of experience and confidence, Dr. Drummond removed Janet's left eye. Janet let out the most awful cry and began screaming for her mother. Aubry could not bear to look at Janet any longer. Still she held on to Janet's hand, which squeezed Aubry's so tight she felt a painful throbbing as the pressure obstructed her blood flow. Janet's hand was clammy. Dr. Drummond went for her right eye, and Janet screamed and turned away.

"You're going to have to restrain her," Dr. Drummond demanded. He grabbed Janet as she tried to scramble away and thrust her down on the table. Aubry momentarily froze. "Restrain her now," Dr. Drummond spoke more forcefully than before. Aubry winced and looked into Dr. Drummond's eyes pleadingly. As if he understood her, he spoke, "I need you to hold her down. Her right eye has to be removed, and I have other patients to tend to. We do not have time for hesitancy and debate. Janet needs you."

Aubry moved towards Janet, who was inconsolable and out of control. She was thrashing about under Dr. Drummond's hold. She started scratching wildly and caught Dr. Drummond on the bridge of his nose. Dr. Drummond withdrew. Aubry pinned Janet down on the table with her chest and both hands.

"No, no, no. Don't. Leave me alone. It hurts so bad. I want my mother."

Janet was still thrashing under Aubry, throwing her arms and legs in all directions. Aubry drew upon all of her strength to restrain the child, and the muscles in her arms and back tensed and then began to shake. Aubry closed her eyes tight, and Dr. Drummond moved in closer. He was about to remove Janet's right eye when she let out a howl that pierced Aubry's ears. It was a howl that didn't sound human. Aubry tensed and concentrated as she bore down on Janet.

Aubry's heart was breaking for Janet. She hated being there and holding her down. She felt it was abusive and unjust. She thought it was the role of a mother or father, certainly not a teacher. She would never forgive herself for being there and playing a role in the removal of Janet's eyes. She would never forgive herself for not being able to keep Janet safe.

Aubry was deeply saddened when she thought about Janet's future. It would be a life where the gift of sight had been given, then taken away. How Janet would struggle to function, to learn and to thrive. What kind of a future could she look forward to? Aubry tried to imagine a future in which Janet was able to come to terms with what she and Dr. Drummond had done. She tried to imagine a future in which Janet would find fulfillment, happiness and love. In this moment, she could not.

Aubry shifted her stance, and as Janet continued to struggle, she steadied herself. Dr. Drummond forced Janet's head toward him. Suddenly, Janet ceased all struggling and went limp. As a precaution, Aubry continued to hold the unconscious child down. She attempted to close her eyes as Dr. Drummond went for Janet's eye. Instead, she found she was curious. Though she was squinting, Aubry could not help but look as Dr. Drummond removed Janet's eye.

The gaping hole was creamy and engorged with a slimy substance that was thick and gooey. Aubry imagined what it would be like to stick her finger in the matter that was left behind. She thought it would be cold and slimy. She was all at once fascinated and entirely revolted. Her stomach churned, and she was nauseous. Her head began to pound, and she turned away and emptied the contents of her stomach on the already crimson stained floor.

CHAPTER EIGHT

It was a little after two in the afternoon when Aubry left Camp Hill Hospital and set out towards her house. After searching for Patrick and her parents on every floor at Camp Hill, Aubry knew she had to go home. Perhaps Patrick had returned home in search of her. She would then check her parents' house to see if they were home.

The debris that obstructed her journey along Robie Street was sparser than she had seen along Kaye Street and towards Camp Hill Hospital. Scattered here and there were pieces of timber, metal and concrete. Aubry saw people walking around looking confused and disoriented. Some of them were bleeding, and some of them were holding a wounded limb or worse yet, a wounded child. Some of them were screaming, and some of them were silent.

As Aubry hurried down Robie Street towards her home, she remembered the horrifying sight of the severed arm with the fingers closed to make a fist, as if holding onto something. So deeply disturbed and distraught was Aubry that she could not stop the tears from silently streaming down, blurring her vision.

Turning off Robie Street and onto South Street, Aubry broke into a full run. The next thing she realized was that she was turning the knob of her front door. Her house was nearly completely intact, the exception being that the window in her bedroom had shattered. "Patrick, Patrick, are you here?" she screamed. She ran from room to room searching for her husband. When, at last she knew that every room was empty, and that she was all alone in the house, she turned and left.

Turning back down Robie Street and towards Inglis Street, Aubry began to feel alone. She really needed her mother and father now. In her head, she was alternating between screaming and praying and she may have screamed out a prayer or two. She could not be sure as she was oblivious to what she was thinking.

Turning up her parents' driveway, Aubry knew she had to calm down. She could not appear this upset in front of them. She stood outside for a minute to gather her thoughts, then took a deep breath and tried the front door. It was still locked. She walked around to the back of the house and noted that, much like her house, the only damage seemed to be a shattered window.

Aubry left her parents' house feeling just a little more alone than before. Somewhere in her head, the distant voice of reason calmly told her that her parents had probably just gone to Point Pleasant Park, or to a friend's house. They're probably just fine; she heard the voice reassure her.

Aubry walked down to the end of Inglis Street and turned on to Campbell Road. The further north she walked, the more damaged buildings she could see. Some were without a roof; some were missing a window, and some had no windows left at all. In fact, the street was littered with shards of glass, many of which glinted in the sun. In another circumstance, this might have been quite pretty, but in this one, it made it difficult for Aubry to see as it created pockets of glare that made her squint and look downward. Just like on Robie Street, timber and metal, as well as concrete and other unidentifiable debris was strewn about.

It wasn't long before Aubry could see that the landscape of Halifax was forever changed. Looking forward, she realized many buildings were simply no longer there. Many trees had been snapped in two and their branches had flown through the air at an alarming speed, impaling everything in their path. The streets were becoming more and more obstructed, and walking was becoming extremely difficult. By the time Aubry reached North Street, she could see that Campbell Road was wet, as were some of the side streets. She had to walk a twisted and winding path to avoid the rubble and puddles.

Strewn about were the contents of the harbor: bits of ships, including a ship's wheel from a voyage cut far too short, a porthole from a venture that ended in disaster; and an odd collection of pottery and bottles whose origins could not be traced. They were the final artifacts that proved that someone had once lived.

Also lying about were herring, mackerel, mussels and clams. Having been tossed haphazardly onto the streets of Halifax, most had already been caught in death's grip. Aubry could see the occasional herring or mackerel struggling against all odds to live, only to make one final, uninspired flap against the wet earth.

As she approached Café Halifax, her hope died quickly. It was gone. There was no roof and no walls. All of it was gone. Piles of brick were randomly distributed. Heaps of furniture and pieces of the walls were also lying about in piles. Aubry rushed to what was left of the café, tears streaming down her face now. "Patrick," she wailed repeatedly. "Patrick, Patrick." She tore at piles and heaps of rubble desperately with her bare hands, throwing aside legs of chairs, pots, broken dishes, pieces of tables, and parts of the orange counter. "Oh, God, this isn't real. Tell me this isn't real," she cried out.

After an exhaustive search, Aubry collapsed in the middle of the destruction. She sobbed and wiped tears away from her eyes with dirty hands. She put her head down in her arms, and with her shoulders and chest heaving, her last tear rolled down her cheek and got lost in the filth of her clothes, or in the mud of a city destroyed, she could not be certain. Then she was done, used up. She could cry no more. She had no more tears to offer.

This is how she stayed, in one used-up heap, exhausted and drained. How long she stayed like this, she could not be sure. Suddenly, sensing she was not alone, Aubry brought her head up. A mutt was running in a zigzag pattern just across the street. Aubry slowly got to her feet and curiously observed the dog. It moved on a bit, then came back. It repeated this several times, and Aubry knew the mutt wanted her to follow it.

She crossed the street cautiously and kept her distance from the dog. It was all black, except for a grey patch that ran the length of its back. There was an urgency in the dog's behaviour that Aubry could feel as she followed it. About a block further down, the dog stopped at the beginning of a cobblestone path. Aubry could see the ruins of a house. At first glance, Aubry could see that the only thing that was intact was a wooden sign inscribed with the name, The Meechams, which now lay at her feet. Aubry picked up the sign and ran her slender fingers over the name.

The mutt urged Aubry forward. Still holding the sign, Aubry walked slowly toward the heap of timber that was all that was left of the Meechams' dwelling. As she reached the main pile, she froze. Dropping the sign, she looked down to see the form of a woman. The woman had on a dirty cream-coloured dress. Aubry could see the woman's arm now and dug to free her hand. When Aubry removed the last piece of rubble, she could see the woman's hand was clasped completely around that of a child's.

Aubry let out a barely audible "Oh" and stopped digging. She was not sure she wanted to see what was under the rubble. The mutt started digging at the child, stopping now and again to bark at Aubry. Sighing, Aubry neared the dog. She could see the exposed hand of the child and part of the child's pink dress. "Oh, a little girl," Aubry said to no one in particular. The dog's ears perked up, as if it were listening to her.

Aubry fell to her knees in the dirt. The dog came closer and started barking wildly, as if to say, "Don't you dare stop digging." She tried to push the dog away. But it would have none of that and pushed and nudged and barked louder still.

Aubry knelt down and went to work again. Instinctively, she knew she must dig. She knew that the dog would persist. When Aubry was finished digging, she had exposed the body of a man, a woman and three small children, all girls. One child, who was maybe about six, was lying next to a brown teddy bear. The bear was missing an eye.

Aubry went to the little girl who lay next to the teddy bear. She lifted up the little girl's exposed and lifeless hand and held it in her own. For the first time that day, Aubry looked death in the face. She held on to the little girl's cold hand, as if holding it might warm it up. Her lip quivered. What destruction had come to Halifax. A tear rolled down Aubry's face as she looked upon the little girl. The girl's blond hair was dirty and knotted and fell just past her shoulders. Aubry touched the girl's chest, where her heart should have been beating, hoping to feel it rise and fall. It did not. She knelt down beside the girl and listened next to her face, hoping to hear even the shallowest of breaths. She heard nothing.

Still holding the little girl's hand, Aubry looked skyward. Clouds rolled north, as if to answer to a question nobody asked. She dug the girl's other hand free and held them both in hers. How tiny, helpless and cold they were. Aubry bowed her head and prayed with the girl, and for the girl. In the silence that found her, she let go of the girl's hands, listened one more time for a heartbeat, and in finding none, said her goodbye and turned away. As night fell, Aubry made her way towards Richmond, forever changed, forever just a little broken.

As she neared Richmond, her heart beat faster. She could see that it was almost all gone. Most of it was flattened and devastated. There was an endless scattering of rubbish and mounds of debris. Unable to come to terms with the state of the district and seeing burnt building after burnt building, Aubry continued on in a daze.

When she tripped and fell, she went hands first toward the ground. This brought her back to reality. Something broke her fall. Whatever it was, it moaned. Realizing that she had landed on top of a badly burnt man whose face had been crushed in, Aubry screamed. As she pulled her right hand away, she took a layer of the man's skin with her. She was on her knees, desperately and frantically trying to peel the man's skin off her hands. He oozed from the freshly opened wound Aubry had inflicted. Yellow and green puss surfaced from the newly created craters, and Aubry gasped as she pulled the last bit of skin off her hands. She heard a muffled cry come from the man. He called out, "Glod felp," followed by a gargling sound that came from his throat. Blood exploded from his mouth and spent itself on Aubry's face.

Aubry struggled to get up. She looked down at the man, who made eye contact with her for the first time. Through swollen lids, the man seemed to be screaming at her. Aubry's pulse quickened, and her breathing became unsteady. She thought that she might pass out on top of the man. She drew in a panicked breath. The sick stench of burnt flesh filled her nostrils and lungs. Aubry coughed and turned away from the man, who convulsed, then was still. She fell onto the man again and then scrambled up.

Aubry took off running deeper into Richmond. About half a dozen strides past the man, she was standing in front of a burning house. She could hear the desperate cries of those trapped within. The cries for help would forever be etched in Aubry's memory, especially as each one fell silent until the last one ceased. What followed was the horrible stench of charred flesh, a smell that Aubry would also never be able to let go of.

Aubry knew she had to find shelter, but it could not be in Richmond; nothing was left. She turned and walked back the way in which she had come, only taking a bit of a different way as she neared the man, whose last words had been, "Glod felp." Yes, God help us all, Aubry thought as she left the carnage in Richmond behind.

CHAPTER NINE

As night fell, Aubry became very weary and anxious to find some shelter. She found herself back at the ruins of Café Halifax. Standing there, Aubry felt the first few snowflakes, as they hit her in the face, each one landing in the dried blood of the dead man.

She heard the sputtering of a motorized vehicle from behind. She turned to see the driver, who was a man who looked to be in his 60s, with a round face, and a kind smile. What little hair he had left was grey, and it punctuated his ears. His belly lifted mightily as he breathed in, and his nose whistled as he let the air go. "My name is Nicholas Brendt," the man informed Aubry. "I am in search of those who need shelter for the night. There is a temporary shelter and medical relief station close by on Chebucto Road. Come, get in. I'll give you a ride."

As the offer was being made, Aubry fumbled for the door handle without hesitation. As she got in, Mr. Brendt advised her that soup was also being served. He told Aubry that all hospitals and temporary shelters were serving soup. Silently, she fell back against the seat. She was tired, oh so very tired, and she was hungry. But mostly she was tired. The two sat in silence the rest of the way.

At the temporary relief station on Chebucto Road, Aubry accepted a bowl of soup and a cup of coffee. She looked around the room on the first floor of the makeshift hospital and observed the many people who looked like they had been through hell and back. One man, whose face was covered in soot and blackened, save for his eyes and mouth, limped around in a daze. Aubry could see pain, shock and disbelief in the faces of many. As she sat on the floor in the far right corner and sipped her coffee, she noticed two volunteers deep on conversation beside the serving table.

Aubry put her coffee down and made her way over to the women. "Hello, my name is Aubry. I have been searching all day. I am looking for my husband, his name is Patrick Putnam. I am also looking for my parents, Francis and Grace MacNicholl. Do you know who I should speak to?" Aubry looked at the two volunteers, her heart full of hope and fear.

"You want to speak to Sadie at the front desk," the first volunteer offered. She was thin and stood about five foot eight. Aubry saw that the woman had an abrasion that started on the left side of her forehead and ran down her face. Her blond hair was thrown loosely into a maiden's bun, and her green eyes were sharp and direct. She was probably in her mid-20s, and Aubry saw she wore no wedding ring.

In another circumstance, Aubry thought, she might have been quite pretty. "Thank you," Aubry said as she turned to leave.

"I hope you find who you're looking for," the first volunteer said, offering Aubry a toothless smile.

Aubry walked out of the makeshift soup kitchen and turned left. At the front desk, an elderly lady sat with a clipboard and pen. Aubry approached Sadie with just the slightest bit of hope. The woman's hair was white, and wavy and all together chaotic. She looked up at Aubry. "May I help you, dear?"

Aubry forced a smile and spoke, "I am looking for my husband and parents. I was advised to inquire at the desk."

"What are their names?" Sadie asked.

"Their names are Patrick Putnam, and Francis and Grace MacNicholl," Aubry offered. Sadie took her pen and with bony fingers she used its end to trace the page on her clipboard from top to bottom. Then she flipped the page with all the effort that an 81-year-old woman with arthritis would have to muster. Her fingers gripped the pen that traced that page, and then the next. Aubry felt a chill as the tar-papered windows offered little protection from the cold December night.

"Sorry, there is no Patrick Putnam, no Francis or Grace MacNicholl either." Sadie looked up at Aubry from behind the desk. "This is only a list of those whose names we know. There are many here without names. I would suggest searching from room to room."

"Thank you," Aubry said in a near whisper, and as she turned away, her heart sank. After searching room by room and seeing horror after horror, Aubry was sickened by what she saw. Feeling empty and cold inside, she began to let her mind take her to a place she had been unwilling to go before. She pondered the possibility of never finding Patrick or her parents. Entering the makeshift soup kitchen again, she went back to her spot in the far right corner and found her nearly empty mug of coffee and half eaten bowl of soup were still there. Aubry bent down and pushed them aside. Then she slid down the wall and slumped into unconsciousness.

She was eight years old and staying with her parents at her great-uncle's house in Sydney. Her great-uncle, Don lived in a five-bedroom house all by himself. She saw herself walk up the short dirt path. She opened the door and stepped inside. The mid-July sun shone from the back of the house and was so bright that Aubry had to adjust her eyes. She looked left, into the empty sitting room. She turned to her right and began to ascend the staircase. She looked down at her feet and stopped. At the landing, she looked to her right and out the stained glass window. Her great-uncle had told her that a church in Sydney had caught fire; the window had blown out and shattered to pieces. Members of the congregation had been offered a piece, and her great-uncle had made his own window out of it.

Although she couldn't really see out of the window, she had always thought it to be beautiful and enjoyed the colours it offered, orange, red, yellow and green. She looked down at her feet again and moved up the next 10 steps. The staircase stopped at another landing and veered to the left for four more steps. Aubry moved up the steps and turned left.

She made her way into the bathroom. The room was large, with a dirty claw tub on the left, and a sink, mirror, and toilet along the right wall. The mirror was covered in a film of dust, and for this reason, Aubry was a blur. She smiled and rubbed a spot clean with her hand. She could see a small part of her face more clearly now. She smiled again, supposing her great-uncle probably never looked at himself in the mirror. She turned away and headed for the door that led to the attic. It was always locked, with the key in the hole. Aubry turned the key and heard a little click. The door creaked open.

She looked down and saw a bird lying lifeless at the bottom of the stairs. Fascinated, she bent down for a closer look. The hummingbird's eyes were open and stared at the wall ahead. The bird's eyes were vacant and sad, as is often the look of the dead. Aubry wondered if the bird had died of starvation after being locked in the attic. She wondered how the bird had got in. Had a window in one of the rooms in the attic been left open? She wondered how long the bird had been dead. From the condition of the body, Aubry thought that the bird had not been there for very long. She closed the door and locked it again, leaving the key in the hole.

She was nine years old and staying with her parents at her great-uncle's house in Sydney. Her great-uncle, Don lived in a five-bedroom house all by himself. She saw herself walk up the short dirt path. She opened the door and stepped inside. The mid-July sun shone from the back of the house and was so bright that Aubry had to adjust her eyes. She looked left, into the empty sitting room. She turned to her right and began to ascend the staircase. She looked down at her feet and stopped. At the landing, she looked to her right and out the stained glass window. Her great-uncle had told her that a church in Sydney had caught fire; the window had blown out and shattered to pieces. Members of the congregation had been offered a piece, and her great uncle had made his own window out of it.

Although she couldn't really see out of the window, she had always thought it to be beautiful and enjoyed the colours it offered, orange, red, yellow and green. She looked down and her feet again and moved up the next 10 steps. The staircase stopped at another landing and veered to the left for four more steps. Aubry moved up the steps and turned left.

She made her way into the bathroom. The room was large, with a dirty claw tub on the left, and a sink and mirror, and toilet along the right wall. The mirror was covered in a film of dust, and for this reason, Aubry was a blur. She smiled and rubbed a spot clean with her hand. She could see a small part of her face more clearly now. She smiled again, supposing her great-uncle probably never looked at himself in the mirror. She turned away and headed for the door that led to the attic. It was always locked, with the key in the hole. Aubry turned the key and heard a little click. The door creaked open.

She looked down and saw a bird lying lifeless at the bottom of the stairs. Fascinated, she bent down for a closer look. The crow's eyes were open and stared at the wall ahead. The bird's eyes were vacant and sad, as is often the look of the dead. Aubry wondered if the bird had died of starvation after being locked in the attic. She wondered how the bird had got in. Had a window in one of the rooms in the attic been left open? She wondered how long the bird had been dead. From the condition of the body, Aubry thought that the bird had been there a while. All that remained other than its eyes were its bones.

Suddenly, the bird turned its head toward Aubry. Its eyes were no longer vacant and sad. They were glossed over with a thickened grey film. It seethed and raged. "How could you leave me here?" it raged on. It lunged toward Aubry's face with its claws ready to attack.

Aubry screamed and opened her eyes. How could she leave Patrick and her parents there, wherever there was? Brushing her hair out of her face, she knew she had to search on.

Leaving the makeshift hospital at Chebucto Road behind her, Aubry trudged north along Robie Street. It was snowing now, light and soft. As she made her way down towards the Commons, which was the city's open park, she could see what she estimated to be 100 tents set up. She would have to search every tent. Crossing the street, she was aware of a baby crying in the distance. In the darkness and deep chill of the night, Aubry shivered. She could feel desperation in the air as she neared the first tent. How completely hopeless the situation was, to bring people here, huddled in tents. The temperature was most certainly below freezing.

From outside the first tent, Aubry spoke. "Is anyone in there? I am looking for my husband, Patrick Putnam, and my parents, Francis and Grace MacNicholl." Aubry could hear rustling from inside the tent and a woman peeled back the flap.

"Sorry, not in here. Do you have any water or food?" the woman asked.

"No, I do not. But they are serving soup at Camp Hill Hospital, and you ought to go there for shelter," Aubry replied.

Making her way from tent to tent, Aubry found many of them to be vacant. She found a tent where there were four young girls and a crying baby who was bundled in a scarf. Aubry was deeply distressed at this discovery. She learned that the four young girls were sisters whose ages ranged from 10 to 17. The baby they had found crying in a house on Campbell Road. A search of the house turned up the bodies of a woman and six children. The girls took the baby and, in search of shelter, had made their way to the Commons. They were exhausted and confused. When Aubry asked about their parents, the youngest girl shrugged her shoulders and began to cry.

Aubry instructed them to make their way to Camp Hill Hospital, just over the hill. The four girls and the baby left the tent and started off towards the hill. Aubry could hear the baby's cries become quieter and quieter as the girls put distance between them and the Commons. A search of every tent turned up more victims, exhausted, shocked, cold and defeated. But Aubry did not find Patrick, or her parents. In fact, Aubry was a stranger among strangers.

She decided to venture towards Citadel Hill. The snow was coming down harder now and accumulating with a vengeance. The nearly 10 centimetres that now covered the ground slowed Aubry's advance. She made her way to the top of Citadel Hill, and looked down on Halifax. She could see every manner of transportation fighting the weather to recover the wounded and dead. People on foot were transporting bodies in carts, horses pulled wagons, and motorized vehicles made their way through the narrow streets. They travelled in all different directions and with varying degrees of speed.

Aubry searched Citadel Hill and found that although more tents had been erected there, people spilled out into the night. Those without the shelter of tents huddled together to keep warm. There wasn't much movement atop the hill. Occasionally, Aubry could hear moaning or crying, but for the most part the Citadel waited in silence for morning, or death, whichever came first. Aubry recoiled at the thought that to many, this meant death by exposure.

Venturing down off the hill, Aubry pushed on. She found herself headed in the direction of Spring Garden Road. As morning approached, and the sun shed new light on Halifax, the immense destruction of the North End and the Richmond District was buried mostly under snow.

Richmond had been almost obliterated. Not a house was still standing. Many had been either washed away by the tsunami that followed the explosion or leveled by hunks of debris that rained from the sky. Some homes caught fire and burned to the ground after being hit by falling debris from the burning Mont Blanc, which sent firebombs hurtling through the air as the result of the enormous winds created by the force of the explosion. Other homes burned as stoves toppled over after the blast.

Bodies lay buried under the snow and rubble, were impaled by telephone poles or simply lay exposed in the streets. Some had been decapitated; some were missing limbs or burned so badly they were beyond recognition. The faces that were not mangled wore expressions of horror, shock, fear, pain, confusion, agony and sadness. Some bodies would be identified, and some would not. Some would be recovered in the hours and days and weeks ahead. Some would be recovered in the spring. Some would be carried away in motorized vehicles or carriages or by recovery workers on foot. Some would be found by strangers, and some would be found by distraught loved ones who either lost part or all of their families. And some would never be found.

And for the living, a long journey lay ahead. For those who were injured badly, surgery would be performed in hospitals, makeshift shelters or in the homes of doctors. Operations would be performed with or without the aid of clean medical supplies and anesthetic. Some would lose limbs, and some would lose one or both of their eyes. Some would have those surgeries while they were conscious, and the lucky ones would pass out midway through the procedure. Many would have shards of glass lying just under the surface of their skin for years, and every so often a shard would break free from their skin, serving as a reminder of that terrible day.

It would take weeks for some to find proper shelter and months of back-breaking labour to clean and clear the city. But the memories were like those shards of glass lying just under the surface of the skin - break free they would, and the haunting truth would stay with the survivors until the day they died. This would be especially true for the children as their childhoods would be forever lost in the debris and the horror that unfolded in the hours following the explosion. Some would never find their parents and never get the chance to say goodbye. Some would have to wait weeks to be reunited with the only family they had left, their fathers or brothers who were overseas fighting in the war.

CHAPTER TEN

As the sun rose in the sky, Aubry found herself at the steps of Nova Scotia Technical College on Spring Garden Road. She took a deep breath and made her way inside. Grateful to be out of the cold, she shivered as she started to warm up.

Doctors, nurses and volunteers hurried about. They were engaged in the task of gathering and packing medical supplies for distribution throughout Halifax. Aubry was approached by a plain-clothed volunteer who looked to be in her teens. The young woman had a haggard look about her that led Aubry to believe that she had been awake for many hours. Her blonde hair was tied back in a bun that had fallen loose in several places, and there were dark circles under her eyes.

Aubry made eye contact with the girl, and the volunteer could see that she was eager to find out anything she could.

"Excuse me, I have been searching all night for my husband and parents. I was wondering if you could tell me to which places you have been shipping medical supplies?" Aubry inquired.

The young girl could see that Aubry was desperate for help and she listed off all the places she could think of. "We have been packing medical supplies bound for Victoria General Hospital, Camp Hill Hospital, the Dalhousie Medical School, and the Young Men's Christian Association on Campbell Road. As well, we have been packing supplies and sending them to any temporary medical aid stations and hospitals that make a request."

Aubry had not realized that there were so many places that she had not checked and decided that she would head to the next closest location, which was the YMCA. It was only a few minutes walk away, but

Aubry knew that in the snow, it would take much longer. She thanked the volunteer and set out in the cold once again.

Aubry found her journey to the YMCA on Campbell Road to be quite exhausting. It was still snowing, and with nearly 30 centimetres on the ground, getting anywhere was nearly impossible. After some time trudging through the snow, which was up to her knees in some parts, Aubry knew she had to stop and rest for a while. But she had to make it to the YMCA first.

Aubry checked at the front desk, and the volunteer consulted her list, which was nearly eight pages long. Again, Aubry was disappointed to learn that Patrick's name was not on the list, and neither were her parents'. She asked about the possibility of staying a few hours for rest and was led to the temporary soup kitchen that was set up in the back room on the first floor.

Aubry gratefully accepted a bowl of lukewarm soup and a cup of water. After finishing both, Aubry lay on the floor and closed her eyes. She fell asleep and stayed that way for more than a few hours. When she awoke, she did so with a start. She had forgotten where she was and how she had got there, and for a few moments, she had forgotten about the explosion. In her confusion, she found herself speaking Patrick's name.

When she came out of her sleepy fog and remembered the explosion, her heart sank. Feeling alone and downtrodden, she swallowed. Her throat and lips were dry. She reached for her cup and, in realizing it was empty, began to cry. It was a silent cry, and no tears came. She stood up and took two steps. But she became light-headed and dizzy and fell to the floor.

Some time had passed when Aubry opened her eyes. She lay in a hospital bed. Her mind played out the last few hours that she remembered, and she could see an image of herself collapsing to the floor. She swallowed, and her throat was no longer dry. She climbed out of her hospital bed and left the room.

She began searching room to room. In the last room at the end of the hallway, the hand of fate wrapped itself around Aubry's and led her inside. There in the bed lay a man sleeping. His chest heaved up and down, labouring under the heavy burden of living. As Aubry neared, her heartbeat quickened, and her breathing became erratic. She became dizzy, and feeling like she was going to pass out again, she steadied herself as she approached the bed.

In the dimly lit hospital room, Aubry gazed at the man in front of her. Feeling whole again, tears ran down her face as she caressed her husband's cheek and leaned in closer. She kissed his lips and whispered his name. Stillness crept into the room, and Aubry was aware of only two things: Patrick's laboured breathing and the beating of her heart. Her body tingled, and she was instantly more alert. She wrapped her hands around his and felt his warmth.

This was how she remained for several hours. The silence was broken when Aubry heard footsteps behind her. Still holding Patrick's hand, Aubry turned slightly and saw a man approach.

"Hello Miss. Do you know this man?" the doctor asked.

"Yes," Aubry replied.

The doctor reached out to shake Aubry's hand and replied, "I'm Dr. Lannigan. "And you are?" he questioned.

Not letting go of Patrick's hand, Aubry said, "I am Aubry Putnam, and this is my husband, Patrick."

Dr. Lannigan withdrew his hand and let it fall to his side. "Wonderful. Patrick was brought to us yesterday, and he was unidentified until just now. He has not regained consciousness, so we brought him here and have been monitoring him ever since. It is my understanding that there are many who have similar stories, without identification and unable to speak for one reason or another. By circumstance, they have ended up in one temporary hospital or another throughout the city. It has been an arduous task to identify countless victims."

Aubry shifted her gaze from Patrick to Dr. Lannigan. In a voice that sounded distant and foreign, Aubry spoke. "Did you say that he has not regained consciousness? Are you saying that he does not hear me, does not know that I am here?"

Aubry stared at Dr. Lannigan, her mouth was twisted and her brows were furrowed. Dr. Lannigan did not respond. "Damn it, tell me," Aubry nearly shouted, betraying the panic in her voice.

Dr. Lannigan chose his words as carefully as he could. "It is impossible to say for sure if Patrick will or will not regain consciousness. With each passing hour, it does become less likely. I have seen coma patients who have opened their eyes after a day, a week, a month. And some never awaken. You must prepare yourself for that possibility. Please come find me if his condition changes." Dr. Lannigan forced a smile and left.

Aubry turned back to Patrick. "Patrick, can you hear me? Darling, open your eyes. Please come back to me," Aubry pleaded, kissing his forehead, his cheeks and his lips. The response was nothing but his laboured breathing.

Something deep within Aubry shattered, and she was suddenly keenly aware of everything. She blinked. Her mind played out the events of the past 30 hours in quick succession. It was like watching a slideshow created by the most depraved mind. She was at St. Joseph's Grade School and she was looking into the face of a child who was blinded by glass and bleeding from her eyes. She was leading the children away from the school, which collapsed shortly after their escape. She was observing the severed arm, with the hand closed and perhaps grasping at something Aubry dared not to know. She was searching Campbell Road and was out in front of the café, now just rubble. She was praying at the side of a dead child. She was in Richmond and falling on a badly burnt and dying man. She was at the Commons, searching from tent to only to find people who were cold and helpless. She was at Citadel Hill, looking down upon the city, whose beauty could not be equaled on any other day, and was now destroyed.

Now, she was observing the last slide. The darkest and most depraved mind seemed to be laughing at the conclusion. She thought of how cruel the world had become and how dreadfully horrible reality was. She could not bear to look at her husband any longer. The realization that all of her dreams, her fantasies, her hopes and happiness might have been destroyed with the explosion was too much. If Patrick never woke up...

Aubry turned away, a storm of emotion bringing about tears that left her nearly blind and disoriented. She ran out of the YMCA and down the street towards the harbour, for what reason she was unaware. Perhaps it was to confront the place where the destruction was born. Perhaps it was to curse the water and scream words, angry words at the place where the horror had begun. Perhaps it was to simply see what was left of where it all began. She needed to be where the explosion had occurred, she needed to be close to the evil that had ripped her heart from her chest and left a gaping hole in its place. She fell to her knees and scrambling back up continued towards the water.

She found herself just at the water's edge. Her footing was unsteady, her mind weak and her heart numb. How much can one person bear and carry with them before they break? Yes, Aubry was broken. She could not, would not, go through life without Patrick by her side. She slipped and fell feet first into the frigid waters of Halifax Harbour. When at last the murky water had closed in around her head, and she could no longer breathe, she opened her eyes and looked up. By the darkness of the setting sun, Aubry could see nothing but the blur of the moon in the sky.

Two arms closed around her waist and pulled her from the freezing water. Although she lay unresponsive, she was breathing. She was gently lowered to the ground and stripped of her clothing. She was then wrapped in a blanket and transported by carriage to an unfamiliar location.

When Aubry awoke several hours later, she was in a stranger's bed. Looking around the room, she could see in the candlelight that she was alone. The memory of losing her footing and slipping into the harbour came to her. It came like a series of flashes. She remembered seeing her foot slip. She remembered the painful chill of the water as it consumed her. She remembered looking up into nothingness. She remembered not trying to save herself. Had she wanted to die?

Judas Wedgewood entered the room, interrupting Aubry's thoughts. "I have brought you some coffee, and some soup. You have come close to your death. You must eat now and regain your strength," he said.

Judas' manner was commanding as he brought the coffee and soup to Aubry's side. Her entire body began to shake. Judas set the coffee and soup on the bedside table and immediately wrapped his arms around Aubry. She started to protest and to push him away.

"Your body is going into shock. You have been through an ordeal and you need to stay warm. I daresay you would have perished had fate not intervened. It was lucky for you I was on a late evening stroll along the harbourfront. My name is Judas." He spoke in a manner that was more formal than he had intended, pulling Aubry closer to him.

For this formality, Aubry was grateful. It put her more at ease, and she allowed herself to be warmed by this stranger, this saviour, her saviour. "I thank you with the most sincere of emotion for saving my life. I am forever grateful, Judas."

Aubry's heart was pounding so hard, she thought surely Judas could hear. Her palms were sweaty, and she shivered. As she took in a huge breath, she noticed for the first time that he gave off a hint of an appealing musky smell. She must be having a physical reaction to the near-death experience she had just had, she thought as she slipped back into a state of one who is unaware.

When she awoke again, she was not sure how long she had been asleep. Her mind was fuzzy, and the recent events a bit of a blur. She did remember that the man who was with her now, whose breath warmed her neck, had said his name was Judas. She remembered that he had saved her life. Her pulse quickened.

He was simply a divine creature. His blue eyes were seductive in their clarity and richness of hue. His strong features and supple lips were animalistic in their raw appeal. His black, wavy hair lay wildly, expressing an indifference that was sexy and honest. Oh, God, I must be delirious, Aubry thought. Is this even happening?

His lips brushed dangerously close to hers, and she could feel his hot breath on her face. She tensed and her lips quivered, no knowing what to do. She shuddered. Judas and Aubry stared at one another in silence. Each searching the other's eyes, looking for something neither of them could express. Aubry fell away once more. Judas let her slip away and got up and blew the candles out. He left her that way, in the darkness and in the silence, allowing her to surrender and to dream.

When Aubry awoke again she was still feeling weak but more lucid. She awoke with Patrick's name on her lips. She decided she would get dressed and go back to the YMCA. She could not help but feel hope and a little joy. For the first time since the explosion, her thoughts were light. She allowed herself to think about the future, beyond today. And she could see Patrick was with her.

She rose out of bed, still nude. She crossed the room to the other side and opened the top drawer of the dresser. The drawer was filled with her undergarments. Her heart jumped. Feeling prickles all over her body, she sensed that she was not alone. She turned around to see Judas standing there. He was enthralled with her, taking in every inch of her. She could see his gaze slowly move up her body and stop when their eyes met.

She should have felt embarrassed, vulnerable and exposed. But she did not. Instead she instantly felt stronger, defiant, and in control. She felt powerful and that exhilarated her. She turned back around and reached for a pair of red panties. She bent over and slipped them on. Judas had a full view of her buttocks.

"I need to see my husband," she demanded. She reached into the next drawer and pulled out some stockings. After putting them on, she turned back around, with her breasts exposed. Her nipples were erect, and the areola around her nipples was darkened and pronounced. If they had been a sentence, they would have ended with an exclamation point.

She let her eyes fall to Judas' crotch and could see his penis was erect through his pants. A damp spot was forming, and for a second or two, she thought she could see movement. She turned toward the closet door to see which dresses hung there. Perhaps she should have been embarrassed or upset with the situation. Maybe she should have felt awkward too. But she delighted in the knowledge of just how much power she held over him. She knew that when the time was right, she would use it to her advantage. She could hear Judas' footfalls and she knew he had left the room.

Upon arrival at the YMCA, Aubry instructed Judas to wait for her outside. She made her way to Patrick's side and, to her bitter disappointment, saw that his condition had not changed. It had now been more than two days since he had been brought here.

Aubry kissed Patrick on the lips and left. Each day for the next week, Aubry did two things; she checked the newspapers to see if her parents were listed as being in one of the many hospitals or makeshift morgues, and she went to Patrick. She alternated between days of extreme strength, faith and resolve and days of weakness, hopelessness and defeat. She would find herself between two mindsets, from holding on to hope for her parents and Patrick, to resigning herself to a life without them. Either she was making plans or she was on her knees crying.

She had not been back to her house on South Street. Instead, she spent her time with Judas. It began to feel like a lifetime ago that she was with Patrick. A part of her mourned him a little bit more each day. With each passing day, Dr. Lannigan's view was less hopeful. Something in Aubry had begun to change. She had become more detached from her own self and everything around her. Perhaps her way of coping was to continue day by day, shutting more and more of her emotions down. It was as though she had to turn off her feelings to carry on. To be sure, she still cried sometimes, but even those tears were becoming less frequent, and when she did cry, it wasn't really her, but some distant her. So it was, with this separation from herself, that she was able to carry on.

CHAPTER ELEVEN

On December 17th, Halifax had gathered at Chebucto Road School to bury the unidentified dead. Of the nearly 2000 killed in the Halifax Explosion, over 200 unclaimed bodies remained, and Catholic and Protestant funeral services were held.

A small wooden fence separated the mourners from the caskets of the unidentified. Thousands of people had gathered to say goodbye. Very few citizens of Halifax were unaffected, if any at all. Of the small number of people who had not suffered the loss of a loved one, only fewer still could hold on to the fact that they did not know someone who had perished. In fact, death was everywhere. If you had not lost a mother, father, child or sibling, you lost a neighbour, a friend or an acquaintance.

Death was all around. It seeped into the soil, the water and the air. On this cloudy day in December, the stench of death blanketed the city. As Aubry looked around at the thousands of mourners, she could see a wide range of emotions. Some people still wore a look of shock and utter disbelief, and some carried with them an immense sadness that seemed to define who they were. Many people looked tired and worn, and some looked devoid of any feeling.

How does Halifax say goodbye to nearly 2,000 people? How can Halifax accept and move on and rebuild? How can Halifax come to terms with what has happened?

As the First World War still raged in Europe, Halifax had been called upon to endure a different sort of war, perhaps every bit as terrible and tragic. Aubry's mind wandered to these thoughts as the Catholic priest concluded his portion of the services.

Aubry could not help but focus on the smaller caskets. Her mind became so fixated on counting the smaller wooden boxes that she did so repeatedly, 30 children in total, whose lives were taken far too early. An incredible sadness threatened Aubry, but she refused to let it take hold. She wondered how many children simply waited for their mother or father to return to them, and how many of those mothers and fathers lay here? How many of those children had no family left to take them in and now resided in foster care or in one of several orphanages.

Aubry barely took note of the Protestant archbishop as he gave his final words. Instead, her mind was reeling, consumed with thoughts that were the consequence of this great tragedy. As the archbishop concluded, Aubry observed the crowd. She searched the many faces for a familiar one, a neighbour, a friend or a colleague. Instead she saw strangers, and many of them, men, women, and children who were all looking for some measure of closure. Some faces betrayed no emotion, and some wore looks of extreme anger. Several mourners wept, mostly mothers and their children.

One woman broke from the crowd and made her way over the grotesque-looking wooden fence. She rushed the caskets, throwing her body on top of one of the smaller ones in a big heap. "Joseph," she wailed. Her body shook and trembled. "Oh, Joseph," she cried as she slid down the side of the casket and collapsed in the dirt in front of Chebucto Road School in a disheartened heap. Then a bearded man in a long overcoat was at her side, ushering her away.

Aubry looked away, not allowing herself to feel any emotion. She was alone and she knew it. As the crowd dispersed, Aubry's thoughts turned to Patrick, and then to Judas. She began to search the crowd for Judas. They had come together and separated from each other shortly thereafter. Aubry had wanted to be alone. Now though, she longed for his company.

As she walked towards the street, she felt a tap on her shoulder. She turned around and looked into the eyes of Judas. "Are you alright?" he inquired, sensing something had changed in her.

She nodded, unwilling to verbalize how alone she felt until just now. She did not wish Judas to know that she was glad for his company. She did not want him to realize that if Patrick never woke up, he was all she had in this world. No she did not want Judas to come to understand any of this, she wasn't ready yet.

As Aubry drew in the deepest of breaths, the stench of death filled her lungs, and her soul. She had accepted that of the over 200 victims that were unidentified and were lined up in those caskets outside of Chebucto Road School; most likely two of those were her parents.

Somehow, in her own shutdown way, Aubry managed to say goodbye to a possibility, a chance. That is not to say that she didn't sometimes see her parents ahead of her in the streets, or in the front pews at church once in a while, only to discover that it was not them, because, to be sure, she sometimes did. But for the most part, she accepted that they were gone.

CHAPTER TWELVE

In the Public Gardens, the flowers were in full bloom. Beautiful and fragrant roses, chrysanthemums, lilies, and daisies opened their petals to greet the midday sun. Children laughed and skipped ahead of their mothers. In the midst of all this sat Aubry, in one of the rows of permanent seating facing the gazebo. The gazebo was white with a red roof. It provided the most beautiful setting for events such as weddings, recitals and class trips. As the sun warmed her face, a smile spread across it. Her blue eyes stared past the gazebo and into nothingness. She was lighthearted and carefree.

She stood up and noticed for the first time how many had come to enjoy the walking paths, duck ponds and gardens. Aubry walked with no destination in mind. She walked through the cast iron gates that bore the words Public Gardens and the city's coat of arms and left the gardens behind. She thought she would let spontaneity be her guide.

She found herself walking along the waterfront. The harbour was just as busy today as it had been when the war started. Close to 150 vessels sought the safety of the Bedford Basin and the convenience of Halifax as a stopping point, travelling to or from Europe. Many foreign vessels spent the night, and sometimes two anchored in Halifax Harbour. The crew onboard these vessels were never allowed to come ashore for the protection of the citizens.

Along the harbourfront, businesses thrived, being the first point of contact for many Haligonians coming home from the war. Men worked at a feverish pace loading and unloading ships. Taking a deep breath, Aubry inhaled the fresh, untainted air. She looked across the harbour towards Dartmouth. Each day, a ferry boat made continuous trips to and from Dartmouth. Aubry had always loved her trips to Dartmouth and thought she might go today.

Instead, she kept walking for nearly a kilometre and found herself outside Privateer's Wharf. Music was coming from within and Aubry couldn't help but dance. In the rhythmic, steady pulse of the city, no one took notice. She swayed her hips back and forth, and spun around in a circle, her arms stretched toward the sky. She felt a simple joy.

It seemed no matter where she was in Halifax, she was not alone. At lunchtime, crowds took to the streets, cafes and restaurants, and this day was no exception. Crowds spilled out into the street, becoming an extension of the restaurant or cafe they were frequenting. A warm breeze made the 30-degree day feel a little cooler. To Aubry, this was home.

When the music stopped, Aubry continued on her way. She found herself at Parade Square. Hundreds of soldiers were gathered in celebration. Aubry went unnoticed as she walked through the joyous crowd. The soldiers were laughing and cheering. Aubry found herself lost in a sea of men, and when one bumped into her, knocking her to the ground, he continued on his way, paying no heed.

Aubry blinked, and the merriment was gone. So was the afternoon sun. She found herself utterly alone and lying in a heap of snow, in total darkness. She exhaled and could see her breath. She shivered and attempted to stand.

That was when the thing with no face pushed her down and began to tear away at her clothes. With seamless effort, her clothes were gone and she lay naked. The beast howled and bent toward her. Her eyes moved from the faceless head down the massive hulk of a body and stopped at the thing's pulsating cock. The tip was red and glistened with drippings. He thrust it in her and cried as he moved it about, violating her.

To Aubry, it was too much. Its massive expanse felt as though it would break her as it moved back and forth, and up and down. The pain it caused was extreme as it spread throughout her entire body, rendering her defenseless, and she could not move. When the beast let out a final cry, Aubry was flooded with his blow and it began to feel pleasurable. Waves of heat crested and broke.

Fingers suddenly entered her and thrust about wildly. More fingers found her clitoris and rubbed rapidly. Together, the thing's fingers moved inside and out, and faster and faster. Her heartbeat fell and rose, and synched with the thrusting and rubbing, and she thought she might be driven to insanity as she had never felt this kind of pleasure.

Her entire body shook and surrendered to the beast. The most powerful of sins washed over her as she screamed and let go. The heat of the beast's pleasure-making was so intense that sweat poured out of Aubry's breasts and midsection, and from between her legs and buttocks.

When she stole a look at the beast's cock, she could see steam rise as yellow liquid exploded and ran down the base of it. The beast moaned as a mouth formed and it was suddenly around Aubry's left nipple, then her right. She could feel the beast sucking and could hear it drinking as it concluded by compelling her breasts dry.

Aubry could feel herself start to awaken. It was in this half-asleep, half-awake state of arousal that Judas entered her. Before she opened her eyes, she could smell him and she could not help herself. The intense heat she felt between her legs could not, would not be denied. She opened her eyes and their lips met for the first time. Judas rolled his tongue around inside her mouth in a way that would later drive her to climax more than once.

She threw herself on top of him and thrust up and down, her buttocks clenched between his hands. She leaned forward and sucked his neck. She threw her body back and forth, faster and faster. When he moaned and neared orgasm, she pulled off of him and let him ejaculate into her mouth.

When they finished, they lay in silence. Aubry's thoughts immediately turned to Patrick. Oh, if he could see her now. Surely he would hate her, now that her soul was stained forever with infidelity and betrayal. She was ashamed, more deeply than she imagined she would be.

As Judas slept, Aubry gazed at herself in the mirror. She saw a darkness in her eyes that she did not recognize. She felt sick to her stomach, and her head hurt. She thought she might vomit. She knew as she frowned at herself that she would have to make a decision. She would either have to go to her husband and stay by him no matter what or to accept that her life was no longer the life she had known before.

What Aubry decided was to accept that her life had changed. She reasoned that Patrick might never wake up. She told herself that she knew she had changed because of the explosion and she had been scarred and had started to shut down. She was anxious to feel emotions again and she reassured herself that she would begin to feel again if she stayed with Judas. In time, she thought, she might actually grow to love him.

It was with these justifications that Aubry proceeded. Judas proved to be a hungry beast in bed. They created a world for themselves as lovers often do, where only the two of them existed. They enjoyed pleasuring each other most days, and often more than once a day. Two sweat-soaked bodies would often lie for hours after the last of the screams were heard, both nude and throbbing. Weeks passed in a haze of pleasure and sex. Aubry and Judas settled into their new life together.

CHAPTER THIRTEEN

In January, Halifax was well on its way to a rebuilding phase. Temporary housing had been built on the Commons and at the Exhibition Grounds on Almon Street. Donations of money and furniture had poured in from Massachusetts, all across Canada and even from as far away as Australia. It was, for the city, a time to remember the immense loss, and a time to be optimistic about the future. People were pushing forward. It was for the city, a new beginning.

It was a new beginning for Aubry as well. On one bright and chilly day in January, Aubry set out for the YMCA. As she approached Patrick's bed, she began to shake nervously. She sat down and took his hand in hers. She fumbled for words that didn't come easily. "Can I say goodbye, without actually saying goodbye?" she asked herself.

"Oh, Patrick, my dear Patrick; if only you had come back to me. Losing you has been harder than I ever thought possible. Seeing you for the first time after the explosion gave me great hope. How I have longed for you to open your eyes, to tell me you love me, to hold me once more."

A tear rolled down Aubry's cheek and fell to Patrick's bed. As she stood up kissed her husband on the cheek, another tear escaped and fell to his lips. Patrick's eyelids fluttered, and his breathing became erratic. Aubry stopped and backed away slightly, her eyes searching his face. Again, his eyelids fluttered, and she could see movement under them. She remained still, holding her breath. Her heart stopped momentarily as she waited in anticipation. Patrick shifted in the bed.

At that moment, she expected him to open his eyes, speak her name and to come back to her. The moments stretched on and became minutes. She began to speak his name over and over and over again.

Each time she spoke it with more emotion than before. She choked back tears as she began to feel again. Memories came rushing back. Something in her changed and she found herself without barriers. And her betrayal struck her like a slap in the face. Her cheeks reddened. Ashamed, she looked away. His fingers moved.

From another bed, a patient coughed. Aubry turned her gaze back to Patrick. The other patient began a coughing fit. Aubry watched and waited.

Patrick lay there motionless. His breathing had steadied, and his eyes had stopped moving. Aubry's heart sank. She sat back down in her chair and took his hand in hers once again. The coughing had ceased. Aubry's world stopped. Sadness washed over her and held her in chains of despair, and with a soul that called out in darkness, Aubry said goodbye to a love that few would ever know.

Exhaling, she was done. She reached into her pocket and brought out the gold locket. She turned it over in her hands and spoke the inscription out loud, "01/02/1917 AM." She laid the locket on the bed next to Patrick and walked away.

CHAPTER FOURTEEN

The Halifax Explosion was an immense tragedy that changed the land-scape of the city and its citizens forever. The loss of life, the damage to the city and the horrors that would remain in the hearts and memories of its citizens for years to come could not be overstated. Through the pain of it all, and despite the loss, examples of miracles and stories of hope and triumph of the human spirit could be told.

One such miracle occurred in mid-April 1918 on a mild and rainy afternoon. Patrick Putnam opened his eyes. He could deduce that he was in a hospital from the patients in the other beds. But he was lacking all other details. He knew not what had happened or what day it was. He felt weak and attempted to speak. Had anyone been leaning in close to hear what he was trying to say, all they would have heard was a series of gasps, followed by a whistle.

A nurse was walking by, and habit dictated that she look his way. When she did, she was astonished to see that he was awake. She forgot all else and went to his side. When, at first he tried to speak, and could not, nurse Melissa Smith understood at once. She went away and came back a few minutes later with some water. Patrick gratefully accepted the water and drank nearly all of it at once. Again he tried to speak, but Nurse Smith could tell it was with a great deal of effort.

"Please take your time," the nurse said gently. Nurse Smith was a formidable presence. She was heavy-set and just over six feet tall, with shoulder-length blond hair, blue eyes and masculine features. Yet when she spoke, her voice was soothing and contained the qualities of a lullaby. Patrick attempted to convey his questions in a simple, plead-ing glance.

Nurse Smith began to explain the events of the last four months of his life, describing the explosion in great detail. As Patrick understood it, on December 6, 1917, the munitions ship, the Mont Blanc and the Belgian relief ship, the Imo had collided in the narrows of the Halifax Harbour. The Mont Blanc was loaded with explosives, wet and dry picric acid, TNT, gunpowder and benzol. Drifting towards Halifax, the Mont Blanc caught fire and at 9:04 a.m., the ship exploded. What followed was a rain of terror, which fell from the sky. Pieces of the Mont Blanc, some ablaze, hurtled through the air. The remnants impaled those it struck, severing limbs and killing some instantly. Those that were ablaze struck buildings and caused many fires on impact, and entire families trapped in their homes were burned alive. An intense wind formed as the result of the pressurized air attempting to seek balance, snapping trees and blowing the glass out of many surrounding buildings. A tsunami also occurred as a result of the enormous blast, and it temporarily emptied Halifax Harbour, spilling the harbour water into the streets.

Most of the damage was found to be in Richmond, which the explosion almost completely leveled. However, surrounding areas were quite heavily damaged, and most buildings in Halifax suffered some damage. In fact, most buildings had some or all of their windows blown out.

Nurse Smith went on to explain how Patrick had been brought in within several hours of the explosion, having been found under the rubble of Café Halifax by rescue workers. Patrick knew at that moment that his businesses were all gone: Halifax Hotel, which was in Richmond; Café Halifax, which sat on the outskirts of Richmond on Campbell Road; and Putnam Cinemas, also on the outskirts of Richmond. He sank back down in his bed and closed his eyes. He heard a distant, unfamiliar voice ask, "How long have I been here?"

Nurse Smith shifted her stance. Telling patients that they had lost time was never easy. She looked down at the floor and found herself unable and unwilling to even answer his question. Still unsure of exactly how she was going to answer his question, Nurse Smith opened her mouth to speak and began, "Patrick..."

From behind her, a surprised Billy interrupted her, "Patrick, it's good to see you. You're looking well." Billy made his way past the nurse and to Patrick's bedside. A much relieved Lily followed close behind. Billy looked into Patrick's eyes and knew from his expression that Patrick recognized him. Billy smiled.

"Billy." Patrick spoke in a voice that was barely audible and cracked and trailed off.

"You rest now. We can speak later," Billy responded, shifting his gaze from Patrick's face down to the end of his bed. He noticed the lack of movement in Patrick's lower body.

Patrick closed his heavy eyes and was gone again. Billy and Lily took turns keeping watch over him. The next day, as the late day sun began to fade, Patrick opened his eyes once more. Lily immediately straightened up in the chair she was sitting in and pulled it a little closer to his bed.

At first Patrick seemed to stare into nothingness, his eyes unblinking. Lily grew more concerned as she stood up and hovered over him. He seemed to be locked in some unknown world, seeing who knew what. Something in Lily knew she would never know.

Patrick blinked and looked up at Lily. She smiled and absentmindedly brushed her grey hair away from her face. Patrick swallowed and spoke, "Lily. Lily..."

Lily was nervous. She was unprepared to speak of Aubry.

"Lily, I am parched. Do bring me some water." Lily breathed heavily and turned to fetch Patrick a drink. "Lily, where's Aubry?" Patrick's question was unexpected. Lily was grateful that Patrick could not see her face and was relieved that he had not seen her reaction. She forced a smile and turned to face him.

Patrick's eyes were closed again. Lily took another deep breath, held it in and let it go. She wondered for how much longer the absence of Aubry could be left unexplained.

For the next several days, Patrick awoke sporadically, and how long he remained awake became unpredictable. Sometimes he would awaken for mere minutes, sometimes for more than a few hours. It was clear to Billy and Lily that Patrick's memory was unreliable. Sometimes, he would awaken and they would have to explain to him all over again why he was at the YMCA. Other times, he would awaken and immediately understand where he was and why. On some occasions, Patrick would lie in his bed nearly completely still. On others, Lily or Billy would find him in his chair or sprawled on the floor between the bed and the chair, unable to make it to either without assistance.

As time wore on, Patrick's confusion lessened, and the time he spent awake increased. He began to regain his strength, little by little and seemed to be getting restless and agitated. On one such morning, several weeks after he had opened his eyes for the first time, Patrick awoke in a most agitated state. He was inexplicably unable to remain still as his legs twitched and took on a life of their own under the hospital blankets.

When Nurse Smith entered Patrick's room with his breakfast, she saw that he was working himself free from the blankets and he seemed to be becoming increasingly upset. She dropped his tray of breakfast to the floor and rushed to his bedside. She tried in vain to calm him down. After several minutes, Patrick began to tire and he began to relax.

Nurse Smith began to clean up the mess she had made on the floor. Something gold under the bed caught her eye and she bent down to pick it up. After she had retrieved what turned out to be a necklace, she stared at it. She thought it was the most beautiful locket she had ever seen.

"Oh my God-Aubry," Patrick pleaded in a voice that was unrecognizable, and he was consumed with desperation as he stretched his hand out to the nurse's. She placed the locket in his hand, cleaned the rest of the mess and left to get Patrick another breakfast tray. When she came back, he was gone.

Patrick took to the streets of Halifax dressed in his pre-explosion clothes, the gold locket in the clenched fist of his right hand, and made his way home. His blue shirt was ripped in multiple places and blood-stained. His black trousers were being held up by a belt with a new hole notched in it. They had been heavily soiled with dirt, ash and debris, but were miraculously not torn. Patrick was still feeling weak as he made his way slowly up Spring Garden Road, onto Robie Street and then onto South Street. To those he passed by, he must have looked out of place and out of sorts. He wore no jacket, and in the mid-April rain, he was wet and cold. Walking like a man three times his age, he was, by all accounts, unrecognizable, having lost 22 pounds and despite his nearly four months asleep, dark circles had formed around his eyes.

When at last he stood in front of his dwelling, he opened and closed his fist around the locket, alternating between daring to look and not having the courage to do so. This was how Lily saw him when she looked out the living room window. She rushed out of the house.

"Sir, I am surprised to see you. Let me help you," Lily said as she took him by the other hand, the one not clutching the locket, and led him inside. Together, they entered the house. Patrick broke from Lily's grasp and started up the stairs. "Aubry," he called. Then he stood at the doorway of his bedroom and on the threshold of his fate. He walked inside and needed to rest. He sat down on the bed, examining the locket once more.

"Sir," Lily said in a tentative tone. Patrick looked up at Lily, his eyes betrayed weariness in his soul. Lily looked at Patrick and wondered how she would find the words.

"Aubry has gone. She came for her belongings many weeks ago." There was a silence that wore between them, followed by an exchange of awkward sideways glances.

"Where?" Patrick pleaded. "Where did she go? I must find her and bring her home." He stood up and let the locket fall to the floor. He started towards the door.

"I fear she has taken up with another," Lily explained. Patrick turned to face Lily. He noted for the first time the extreme lines and wrinkles that had taken over her face. No doubt the explosion had added more to those.

"Where did she go? And with whom has she taken up?" Patrick demanded. There was something in his eyes that scared the hell out of Lily, something she had never seen before, and although she had sworn to herself that she would never tell Patrick where Aubry had gone, she immediately confessed.

"She is with Judas Wedgewood, living along the Northwest Arm. But the exact address, I do not know." It was true; Lily had not wanted to know where Aubry was living.

"Judas," Patrick spat the name with a rage as such that Lily had never witnessed before. "Bring me a driver; I must go there at once."

Lily turned away and barreled down the stairs. Patrick barely noticed the heavy thump, thump, thump of Lily's footfalls. He went to the closet, found what he was looking for and put it in the pocket of his trousers. Despite feeling dizzy, Patrick steadied himself for the impending confrontation. Hatred welled up and took over, becoming his master.

In a matter of minutes, he found himself outside his house, ready to take a seat in his carriage. Billy looked away from Patrick, feeling uneasy about what was to occur. He knew the past that lay between the Wedgewoods and the Putnams. This would be Patrick's time to exact revenge. As the horses pulled away, the rain began to come down in torrents. The horses snorted, and clouds of steam poured from their nostrils. With each turn of the wheels, Patrick became more vengeful and more full of rage.

In front of Judas' house, Patrick scrambled out of the carriage. He instructed Billy to leave. Feeling uneasy and knowing he should not leave Patrick in his present condition, Billy reluctantly turned the carriage around and pulled away. He understood the rage in Patrick's heart, but doubted his employer was strong enough for what was to come.

Judas had heard the carriage approach and burst from his house. "What a fool you are," Judas scoffed. "Why did you come here?" A wicked smile crept across his face.

The silence stretched as they locked eyes. Years of pain and torment spread through Patrick like a wildfire through a forest, and he burned with rage.

"In the name of my father, I have come to even the score," Patrick said, seething.

"Ha! Your father, he was weak," Judas said mockingly. "Only the strong survive, Patrick, only the strong," he warned.

The rain came down faster still, and it beat hard on Patrick's face, nearly blinding him. He blinked and saw clearly before him the man whose father had killed his own. He could see in Judas' face, his father, Nathaniel Wedgewood, and that enraged Patrick further.

His memory took him back to the day of his father's death. Patrick had been waiting impatiently at Pier 7 for his father to return from a business trip. The boat that his father had taken Nathaniel Wedgewood out in, the Lady Maria, had been scheduled to arrive 3 o'clock. It was now nearly two hours late, and Patrick paced the waterfront. He did not trust Mr. Wedgewood and knew the man would stop at nothing to control the proprietary interests of Halifax. When he had tried to buy all Putnam holdings in Halifax, Patrick's father had refused.

Patrick's father had invited Mr. Wedgewood aboard the Lady Maria in an effort to talk business and put an end to the dispute. When the Lady Maria arrived back at Pier 7, only one man had survived. Patrick knew the account of the business trip; the accidental drowning Mr. Wedgewood recounted was a blatant lie. Yet he could prove nothing.

With all the honour that a good man could muster, Patrick had vowed to keep his father's businesses going. He put all of his efforts into ensuring that the businesses were profitable and thrived. Throughout the years, he proved to be a successful businessman. But deep down inside, his hatred for the Wedgewoods grew, and he was secretly consumed by it. It was with him everywhere he went, and it tainted his soul.

Now with all that hatred, he lunged at Judas, leaving his feet. He came down hard on his enemy, knocking him to the ground. Judas scrambled back to his feet and spat in Patrick's face. Patrick swung his fist and caught Judas in the jaw. Judas opened his blood-filled mouth and spat out a tooth.

Thunder cracked overhead. Judas threw himself at Patrick and took him to the ground; the two rolled around, each trying to get the upper hand. Judas' knee came up hard into Patrick's crotch, and Patrick fell backward. Judas got to his feet and stood over a moaning Patrick. Breathing hard, Patrick struggled to his feet. Judas threw a punch to Patrick's nose that landed with a whack. Patrick's nose burst and blood gushed and ran down his face and pooled at his mouth. He dropped to his knees. His eyes stung and watered, so that his vision was compromised. Judas' elbow came down on Patrick's shoulder with such force that Patrick could feel the bone dislocate.

With his left hand, Patrick fumbled in the pocket of his trousers. His hand found the handle of his knife and he tried in vain to pull it from its sheath. At the same time, he struggled to stand. He gasped and grunted as he got to his feet. Judas balled his hand into a fist and prepared for another blow.

A figure stood in the doorway of the Wedgewood's house. Patrick stole a glance and in a moment, he forgot where he was. His eyes met Aubry's. He could read the look of shock and horror on her face. His eyes moved down to her swollen mid-section. How much pain, how much rage and how much sadness could one person handle? For Patrick, this was it. Something in him died.

Aubry rushed toward the two men. As Judas swung at Patrick, Aubry threw herself in between. "Judas, stop, you're going to kill him." She screamed. Whack. Judas' blow struck Aubry sending her down, and despite the pain in his shoulder, Patrick wrapped both hands around Judas' throat and began strangling him. Aubry was still on her knees, caught between the two dueling men.

Judas' eyes were bulging, and he struggled to breathe. His right arm struggled forth in an attempt to knock Patrick away. At the same time, Aubry struggled to get up and was once again between the two men, just long enough to catch Judas' flailing arm. Judas' elbow caught Aubry in the midsection and she was knocked aside, collapsing to the ground. She cried out, holding her swollen belly. Tears sprung from her eyes.

Patrick released his hold on Judas and fell down beside Aubry. He could see blood soaking her dress from between her legs. The blood pooled underneath her. She looked into Patrick's eyes and whispered, "Oh God, Patrick. I am so sorry. So sorry." She began to sob.

Patrick tried to speak but could not find his voice. Instead, he mouthed the words "I love you, beautiful," and Aubry understood.

Aubry and Patrick had not noticed that Judas had retrieved Patrick's knife, which had fallen out of his pocket and onto the ground. Judas plunged the knife into Patrick's back, and he collapsed by Aubry's side. Horror-stricken, Aubry gazed into her husband's eyes, searching for some unknown reassurance. But his eyes went blank and stared straight ahead. His body went limp. And he ceased all movement.

"Patrick, can you hear me? Don't you die on me," Aubry screamed, "Oh, Patrick, -no -no -no," Aubry's heart sank. There was a quiet that came, save for the sound of the rain. Soaked and still bleeding from between her legs, Aubry's soul bled too. Weakened from the struggle and blood loss, Aubry said, "I love you too, Patrick," and passed out.

Judas spat on Patrick and pulled the knife from his back. He wiped the blade on Patrick's shirt and shouted at the sky in delight. With that, he fled.

Just then, Billy had decided that he must go back and he turned the carriage towards Judas' house. When he saw the river of blood-stained rainwater running down the street, he grimaced. Approaching the house, he tried to prepare himself for what he would find. He tried to reassure himself that Patrick and Aubry were okay. He wanted to believe that the blood he saw belonged to Judas.

But when he pulled up in front of Judas' house, his worst fears were confirmed. He leapt from the carriage and ran to Patrick's side. He knelt beside his boss and checked to see if he was breathing. He was not. He checked for a pulse. There was none. What he saw in Patrick's eyes was the same look that Aubry had seen, the vacant look of the dead. Billy shook his head.

In shock, he went to Aubry. He could see the terrible, telling blood-stain that had spread from the front of her dress at the midsection and soaked through and down to her knees. Billy shook. Aubry moaned and opened her eyes just long enough to see Billy hovering over her, and her eyes closed again.

"Shit," Billy said to himself. He put his arms gently under Aubry and lifted her up. He placed her in the carriage and covered her with his jacket. As the rain started to subside, one thought troubled Billy. Where was Judas?

Billy drew the carriage up in front of Camp Hill Hospital and sprang from the driver's seat. He lifted Aubry, who was motionless but still breathing, out of the carriage and rushed her into the hospital. A nurse immediately took in the scene of a bloodied man holding the nearly lifeless body of a woman, who appeared to be pregnant and who was even more bloodied. The nurse ran for a bed. In mere moments, Aubry was taken from Billy and rolled away.

CHAPTER FIFTEEN

In the days that followed, Aubry began to come around. She slowly began to find her strength, at least her physical strength. She would often weep and find herself in dark places where no hope could be found. Instead, there was hatred and evil and sadness. In those dark places, she wondered why she had to bear the burden of carrying on. She wondered why God had taken her parents, her husband and her baby.

Often in these dark places, she would see the face of evil. Always in her vision, it was the face of Judas. He would grin and laugh and that laughter haunted her in sleepless nights and sorrowful days. She came to believe that this evil had saved her from drowning in the harbour that fateful night so that it could take hold of her spirit and never let it go. She also came to believe that the only escape was death.

She wrestled with such thoughts day and night. Sometimes she believed that taking her own life was the only acceptable end. How could she carry on in a world that was empty, a world that she had created for herself? All of her choices brought her to this conclusion. She went so far as to attempt to determine how she would do it. She debated the effectiveness of such means as hanging herself, overdosing on medication or slitting her wrists.

On her wedding anniversary, July 18, 1918, Aubry found herself in the darkest of places. She awoke just as the sun was coming up in a clear blue sky. She had just had a nightmare and was gasping for breath and clammy all over. Even her bosom was soaked, and her heart was racing.

As she attempted to calm herself down, she heard clattering coming from the kitchen. Lily was preparing fresh coffee. For this, Aubry was grateful. After being released from Camp Hill Hospital, Billy had implored Aubry to come home. Although she didn't think it was a good idea, she felt she had nowhere else to go. Lily had acted strangely around her at first but she was starting to come around.

Aubry's head was pounding. She slipped out of bed and headed for the bathroom. She slipped out of her nightclothes, and they quietly pooled on the floor at her feet. She turned the water on and stepped inside the tub. As she realized what day it was, tears rolled down her cheeks, and she lost all grip on reality. There she sobbed for nearly 30 minutes, even though the water had gone cold more than 10 minutes before.

"Oh Patrick...Patrick, I need you so badly. I am not sure if I can do this alone. If you're with me somehow, show me a sign." Aubry closed her eyes. No sign came.

"Mrs. Putnam, are you alright in there?" came the concerned voice of Lily.

Aubry opened her eyes and stood up. She reached for a towel and climbed out of the tub. "Yes. Thank you," she replied.

A few minutes later, Aubry was in the kitchen sipping on her coffee. In front of her were her wedding photos. She flipped through them, stopping at the one where a shadow hid half of Patrick's face. How haunting it was.

Aubry tormented herself with thoughts of happier times. She ridiculed herself for the choices she had made. How could she carry on in a world without Patrick? She had told herself once that she could not. How could she ever forgive herself? He had practically died at her hand. How could she move on? She was so alone. Judas had taken everything from her, and it was by his hand that her unborn child had died.

She shook her head and let it all go. Months of pain and anguish, memories that would not stop tormenting her rushed her all at once. Her heart thumped, her head pounded, her palms were sweaty and she was cold, so very cold. It all came at her at once, flooding her as a river might overspill its banks.

She could not breathe. She rushed up the stairs and into her bathroom. Something compelled her as she grabbed all the pills in sight and ran into her bedroom and slammed the door. She wedged a chair under the door knob and threw herself on the bed.

That's when her nightmare suddenly came to her. Only it wasn't really a nightmare. In her dream, she saw Patrick in their bed. He was beckoning her to come to him so that he could make love to her.

His rich blue eyes looked into hers and he called for her to come home. "Come to me beautiful, I have missed you. Our time to be together has come. I am waiting for you. When we are together, all is as it should be. I forgive you, beautiful." He held out his arms for their embrace.

"Just hold on for one moment. I am coming, Patrick. I am coming home," Aubry said. All-consuming was their love, and for the first time in a very long time, Aubry felt whole and completely at peace. Tears of pure joy rolled down her face. "Just hold on for one moment. I am coming, Patrick. I am coming home," she repeated. Aubry popped pill after pill from her bottles into her mouth and swallowed.

The last voice she heard as she closed her eyes was Patrick's, and he was saying, "I forgive you, beautiful."

It was all she had ever wanted to hear, and in its own way, the love they shared and what they had been through together, led Aubry to this point, lying on the bed, arranging to be with Patrick, and it was beautiful.

The silence that followed was also for a moment quite beautiful. Then, from the other side of the door came the frantic screams of Lily. She had heard Aubry's excited voice call out to Patrick with the promise of forever, the promise of, "Just hold on for one moment. I am coming home, Patrick."

Lily pounded on the door with her right hand balled up in a fist. In her left hand was the photograph of Patrick's face overcast by a shadow. "Aubry, Aubry open the door. Open the door, Aubry. Come on, can you hear me?" Lily feverishly pounded on the door and tried the knob, nothing.

In a few minutes, Billy was standing outside of the door next to Lily. They were banging on the door and desperately trying to gain entry. Billy twisted the door knob, which stopped abruptly in mid-twist.

"Aubry, open the door," Billy demanded. He threw his shoulder into the door, which shook it in its frame. Still it did not open.

On the other side of the door, Aubry lay still in the bed. She could see Patrick's silhouette and she made her way towards him. He was standing in the distance, arms outstretched, waiting to embrace her. She smiled and started to run towards him. He smiled back, and she knew everything was going to be all right. When they were together, everything was as it should be.

Aubry had always believed strongly that people got one great love in their life, and only one. She believed that in love, there were no second chances. With that belief there was a great responsibility to follow your heart and protect that love, even if it meant going to the ends of the Earth and back.

Aubry neared Patrick. No, she had not protected her one great love in life as she should have. She had not gone to the ends of the Earth and back, but she would leave this Earth for her great love. This was her chance to protect it. Her arms opened wide to accept her husband's embrace. Aubry's heart was unburdened for the first time in a very long time, and she was letting go. Her spirit was preparing for a journey. She drew in a huge breath, and there was a pause.

The pause lasted for quite some time. Patrick looked into Aubry's eyes and at that moment, when the lovers touched, they became one. An intense heat ran through Aubry, and a bright light radiated off both of them.

Aubry foamed at the mouth and spittle ran down the side of her face. She coughed and in one glorious life-affirming moment, she threw up a cocktail of pills, coffee and sputum. She heaved, and the vomit kept coming, exiting her body with alarming force and at an equally alarming rate.

Billy burst through the door in time to see the last of Aubry's heaving and hitching. He took in the scene, observing several pill bottles lying in the bed, all of which appeared empty. On the floor next to the bed was Aubry's vomit. He could see several telling pills that had not had enough time to be digested.

With no time to waste, Billy bounded down the stairs and prepared the carriage. Shortly thereafter, he was back in Aubry's bedroom. He cautiously removed Aubry from the bed. She was conscious but just barely. He set her down in the carriage. Lily was close behind with a blanket and a bag with some of Aubry's belongings, which she had hastily thrown together.

Lily climbed in the carriage in order to keep an eye on Aubry. The ride to Camp Hill Hospital was the longest ride of Lily's life. Along the way, Aubry coughed and sputtered and shifted her position slightly. A few times, Aubry's breathing became intense as she drew in large breaths and released them. Usually this was followed by such a pause in Aubry's breathing that it startled Lily.

CHAPTER SIXTEEN

So many nights Patrick came to Aubry in her dreams. His presence was so real she almost felt as though he had come back to her. In a way he had. In the lonely days that followed her overdose, she welcomed his presence.

In some dreams, Aubry and Patrick would make love like they had never parted ways. In other dreams, they would go about their lives in an almost mundane fashion. Aubry was no longer suicidal. Knowing that Patrick had forgiven her and feeling his presence once again gave Aubry a reason to carry on and a new outlook on life.

To Billy and Lily, Aubry's new outlook was a source of concern. While they were thankful that Aubry was no longer a threat to herself, they wondered if she was truly grieving for Patrick and moving on.

The fateful day when Judas and Patrick had fought resulted in Aubry being taken to Camp Hill Hospital. While she was recovering, Billy had made arrangements for Patrick's burial. All that Aubry had to do was to visit Patrick's grave marker at Mount Olivet Cemetery. But she had chosen not to. In fact, she had never spoken of the terrible day in which she lost her husband and her unborn baby. She had also never mentioned Judas' name.

In particular, Billy had a difficult time with Aubry when she recounted a dream she had just had in which Patrick came to her. She spoke so animatedly, and Billy could see a spark in her eyes that was only present when she spoke of Patrick. He did not have the courage to confront her, so he would always show support with a nod and a smile. Indeed, Billy did not think it was healthy for Aubry to go on this way, but he liked to see her happy, and it did his heart good.

After one such dream, Aubry opened her eyes and she could sense she was not alone. A breeze blew her dark red curtains just ever so slightly, which she thought was strange as she had recalled closing the window the night before. One thought kept on resonating with her, as she heard Patrick say, "Make it count." Aubry wished she could understand what Patrick was trying to tell her, and although she searched for other signs or indicators that she was not alone, she received none.

She rose and readied herself for the day. Still she could hear Patrick's voice, which was saying in her head, "Make it count." "Make what count, Patrick?" Aubry asked out loud. She was sipping her second cup of coffee and finishing her breakfast. Lily shook her head at Aubry's question as she began to clear away Aubry's half-eaten pancake. Aubry took no notice. At least she's eating better, Lily thought as she put the plate on the counter.

Aubry sighed and finished her coffee. "I am going out today, Lily," she announced.

"Very well, I will have Billy bring the carriage around," Lily replied.

"No need," Aubry said. "It is a lovely day for a walk, don't you think?" She didn't wait for an answer.

She set out at about 9 in the morning. As she closed the front door behind her, she looked skyward. Yes, what a beautiful day for a walk, she thought. She knew not where she was going. She only heard Patrick's voice in her head again. "Make it count."

She walked down Inglis Street and stopped just outside her parents' home. The house was shuttered and quiet, as it had been since December 6, 1917. A long time ago Aubry's heart had stopped fluttering with hope as she made her way to this destination. Yet she was compelled to go there from time to time.

The green paint was beginning to peel off the outside of the house, and the grass had become overgrown a few months ago. Aubry made her way around back. Tar paper still covered the blown-out window.

Aubry knew it was time to stop neglecting the house. She knew her parents were not coming back and she knew under the peeling paint and the overgrown grass, the house was still hers, and her house was still the same. Yes, she would tend to this, later.

She continued on her way to the bottom of Inglis Street and turned left onto Campbell Road. The city truly was rebuilding, and Aubry's heart soared. She knew this was her rebuilding phase as well. She knew she was on the cusp of discovery. Patrick's voice was growing louder, and his message more frequent. He was leading her somewhere, she knew it. She could feel it. She was exhilarated and excited. She knew he was about to reveal the meaning behind his message.

Aubry continued to walk north on Campbell Road. With her anticipation growing, her pace quickened. She turned left onto Cogswell

Street, then right onto Brunswick Street. She found herself outside of the The Brunswick Street Orphanage.

She knocked on the front door and waited. Moments had passed when a woman who looked to be in her mid-40s opened the door. "May I help you?" she inquired, sizing Aubry up.

Marguerite looked like a serious woman. She wore an expression that was both stern and disapproving. At nearly six feet tall, she quite towered over Aubry.

"My name is Aubry Putnam. May I come inside?" Marguerite looked hesitant for a moment. Aubry smiled and shuffled her feet. Marguerite opened the door and allowed Aubry entry.

"What is the purpose of your visit? Are you looking for someone? You do not look familiar to me. Have you been here before?" Marguerite peppered Aubry with questions as she led her to her office on the left.

Marguerite took a seat at her desk and shuffled some papers. All at once, Aubry understood why Patrick had led her to the Brunswick Street Orphanage. Or at least she thought she did. Aubry took a seat on the wooden chair on the other side of the wooden desk.

"I am interested in volunteering my time. I can cook, clean and sew. As well, my background is in teaching. I would like to know how I can become involved in the care of the children," Aubry said.

As Marguerite regarded her, Aubry could see the stern, disapproving look disappear from the other woman's face and her expression soften.

"We do have many children in our care, and could use a volunteer to help with the day-to-day tasks. How many hours a week would you be interested in offering?" Marguerite asked.

Aubry considered the question for a moment. "I am available for as many hours as needed," she said.

Marguerite considered Aubry's offer. "Perhaps you would like a tour. I think it best that I show you around. After that, we will discuss your request further." With that, she rose from her chair and gestured for Aubry to follow her.

She led Aubry down a hallway and to the left, there was a sitting room where three children were playing with dolls. Marguerite approached them, and Aubry followed.

"Children, this is Aubry," Marguerite said.

Aubry smiled and lowered herself to their height, making eye contact with each one in turn. "It is a pleasure to meet you," she said.

"This is Trudy, Alice and Elizabeth," Marguerite announced. The children did not speak but went back to their play.

"There are 25 children living here. Sixteen of them came to us after the explosion. There are some truly sad cases. We do our best to provide not only the necessities in life, but also to provide a home that is stable and nurturing. Before the explosion, we cared for children who for one reason or another were orphaned. The explosion brought us more children who were not only orphaned, but who were in need of medical care. It has been very challenging to say the least. The individual care these children require has been difficult. Tending to their physical and psychological needs has required the staff to work longer hours and has taken a great deal of patience. As I have said, we do our best to not only provide the necessities in life, but also to provide a home that is stable and nurturing. Certainly we could use more help." Marguerite looked at Aubry to see if she could read her expression. She could not.

Next, she led Aubry to the kitchen at the back of the house. The kitchen was large and contained five wooden tables, two on the right and three on the left. There were five chairs at each table. The floor, which was the same hardwood as the rest of the house, was spotless. At the sink were two women, one washing dishes and the other drying.

Marguerite introduced Aubry. "Jean and Patsy, this is Aubry. Jean has been working here for five years and Patsy started just after the explosion."

"Hello, Aubry," Patsy said, offering a smile.

"It is nice to meet you," Jean said, taking a plate from Patsy and drying it with the red and white checkered drying cloth she held in her hands.

Jean and Patsy looked like they could have been sisters. Jean had dark brown hair which she wore pulled back in a long braid. Her brown eyes were huge and gentle. She stood about the same height as Aubry and was quite thin. Aubry guessed that she was perhaps 35.

Patsy stood a few inches taller than Jean. She had light brown hair which was quite a bit shorter than Jean's, falling just above her shoulders. Patsy too had brown eyes that held a kindness that put Aubry at ease. They both wore plain blue ankle-length dresses.

"The children are out back playing just now," Patsy informed Marguerite and Aubry.

"Come, let me show you the rest of the place," Marguerite said. Aubry followed Marguerite to the back of the kitchen and up the stairs. There were five bedrooms and one bathroom. In each of the bedrooms were five single beds all neatly made up with the same yellow linen. Each bedroom also had the same beige curtains and contained three dressers apiece. Aubry could see the conformity throughout but also noted the personal items in each room. Toys and stuffed animals were neatly placed beside each bed. Aubry could not help but notice the lack of books.

Overall, she found the neatness and order of the house to be very pleasing. Indeed, this was where she belonged. She immediately felt that her contributions could make a difference and she knew she wanted to help in any way Marguerite saw fit.

Marguerite interrupted Aubry's thoughts. "Come back tomorrow morning at 8 o'clock. I will have a dress waiting for you, and you can meet the rest of the children. That is if you are still interested in offering your time to us. We will see how the children get along with you, and by the end of the week, we will discuss the possibility of your future here."

Aubry was delighted with Marguerite's offer. "I will be here at 8 o'clock," Aubry confirmed. With that, Marguerite escorted Aubry to the front door and bid her farewell.

"I am making it count, Patrick," Aubry said, smiling as she made her way home. She was all at once nervous and excited for the morning. She looked forward to meeting the rest of the children. She knew her future had a whole new meaning now. She felt a joy in her heart that she had missed since her days of teaching.

CHAPTER SEVENTEEN

The next morning at 8, Billy brought the carriage to a stop outside the Brunswick Street Orphanage. Aubry thanked him, stepped down from the carriage and knocked on the front door. Marguerite opened the door and smiled at Aubry.

"Good morning. You are right on time. I like that in a volunteer," Marguerite said warmly. "The children are eating their breakfast just now. Come inside."

Aubry followed Marguerite into her office. Marguerite presented Aubry with a blue dress like the ones Jean and Patsy had been wearing the day before

"Once you have put this on, meet me in the kitchen. I will introduce you to the rest of the children," Marguerite said, leaving Aubry to change and closing the door behind her. When Aubry had changed, she made her way to the kitchen.

She looked around at the children eating their breakfast of porridge. Twenty five children with 25 clinking spoons made the most wonderful music Aubry had ever heard. Marguerite called for everyone's attention. "Children, I would like to introduce you to Aubry. She will be helping out this week. Please treat her with the same respect you show the rest of us."

Marguerite took Aubry around to each child at the first table. Aubry was introduced to five children, Charles, Joseph, George, Henry, and Walter. The boys were more interested in their porridge but acknowledged Aubry with a nod or a smile.

"I am so happy to meet all of you," Aubry said with a smile.

At the next table, Aubry was introduced to five girls, Ruth, Marie, Florence, Catherine and Janet. Aubry's heart skipped a few beats as she gazed upon Janet Moore. For a moment, time stood still as Aubry's thoughts ran feverishly. She had not realized that Janet had ended up orphaned and living at the Brunswick Street Orphanage. Why hadn't Janet's parents found her? Where were they? Were they dead? Why was Janet here? Didn't she have any relatives she could stay with? How long had she been here?

Aubry could see loneliness in Janet's face that the girl did not need eyes to convey. She did not know what to say. She was eager to find out about Janet's circumstances, and yet the guilt she felt prevented her from asking. She could not find words to express her feelings. In time though, she wanted to tell Janet how sorry she was.

"Hello Janet, how are you?" Aubry asked tentatively. Janet cocked her face in Aubry's direction and recognizing her voice replied, "Miss MacNicholl, I am alright." Janet went back to her porridge. Aubry went around the room and met the rest of the children. By this time, the children had finished their breakfast, and Aubry was called upon to clear away the dishes and tidy up.

For the rest of the week, she arrived every morning at 8 o'clock and stayed until 6 o'clock. When the last of the supper dishes were cleared and cleaned, Billy would be waiting outside for her. Most of her days were spent getting to know the children and helping out with the cooking and the cleaning.

Aubry learned that Charles had lost his father in the war, and his mother had simply left him and his brothers George and Henry at the Brunswick Street Orphanage because she could not care for them. She learned that Walter had lost both his parents in the explosion. As well, he lost four brothers. She learned that Janet's parents had perished also. Each story was as heart-wrenching as the one before.

In the week that passed, Janet had not said much to Aubry, and although she felt awkward around the child, Aubry was determined to reach her. Aubry had explained to Marguerite, Patsy and Jean about the day she was with Janet while Dr. Drummond removed her eyes. Although she left out the part where she physically held Janet down, Marguerite could see that Aubry was struggling to get past that day. She wondered if it was not in Aubry's best interest if she didn't come back. At this suggestion, Aubry's heart sank. She practically begged for one more week, and seeing the sincerity in her eyes, Marguerite agreed.

By the end of the second week, Marguerite could see all the children responding to Aubry. All of them, that is, except Janet. Marguerite weighed the positive and the negative and decided that Aubry's contributions were beneficial and she offered her a volunteer position for as long as she wanted, with the hope that Janet too would eventually open up to her. Aubry thankfully accepted the position.

As the next few weeks drew to a close, she had settled in nicely with the children. As September neared, and the new school year was about to start, Aubry had a decision to make. She was quite conflicted because she wanted to return to teaching; it was her passion. Yet, she felt strongly that she was needed at the Brunswick Street Orphanage and she could not entertain the thought of leaving. So with a heavy heart, she made her decision not to return to teaching.

As a way of satisfying her love of teaching, Aubry suggested to Marguerite that she teach the children life skills. This would be for a few hours on Saturdays and would include topics such as cooking and sewing. Marguerite thought it was a wonderful idea.

CHAPTER EIGHTEEN

On the first Saturday of life skills, Aubry brought her sewing supplies and some linen. She sat before 24 children and threaded enough needles for all the children and herself. As she looked around the room, she noticed that Janet was absent. "Does anyone know where Janet is?" she asked the children.

"She is up the stairs, in her room," replied Charles.

"Thank you, Charles," Aubry said. "I am going to get Janet. I will be back in a few minutes," Aubry said reassuringly. She left the room and made her way to the back of the kitchen and up the stairs. In the second bedroom on the left, Aubry found Janet. She was sitting in a corner with her head down.

"Janet, come join us in the sitting room," Aubry said as she smoothed out her plain blue dress. Janet remained silent. Aubry went to her and sat down next to her on the floor. She hardly knew what to say next, and the silence wore on. Aubry shifted nervously.

"You know I wake up screaming in the middle of the night, and all I see is darkness," said Janet. "In my dreams I can still see, and what I see are the faces of my mother and father. They are smiling at me and sending me off to school. Then I see the ship on fire in the harbor, and my world goes black, and I wake up screaming. If I could cry, I am sure I would.

"Sometimes, in my dreams they are calling me, and I can hear father say, 'Come with us, Janet. It's time now to go.' I never know where we are going and I never care. Then I wake up screaming and I remember that I am here, in this bed, in this room, in this place. And where are they? I don't know where they are; they are dead. And then I hear their voices again and I think they want me to come with them now."

Janet coughed. "For weeks after he took my eyes, I thought about two things only. The first thing I thought was, why me? The second thing I thought was mother and father would not want me anymore because now, I am ugly. I think people don't stand the sight of me anymore because I am ugly. I waited for mother and father to come." Janet's voice trailed off for a minute.

Suddenly, her voice became angry, "Maybe it is better I can't see. I can't see what I look like now, which is good. And I can't see the bad stuff in this world either. I can't see the pain and suffering and I can't see the evil. Do you know what that's like? No you wouldn't; you can still see the pain and the suffering and the evil. I pity you."

Aubry sat up straighter next to Janet. She was stunned. Everything was worse than she thought, much worse. She knew what Janet was feeling. She had been in a dark place too. But she hadn't realized Janet ate, breathed and lived with such a tremendously bleak outlook. She knew she had to find a way to reach Janet but she could not imagine what she could possibly say.

Aubry leaned in closer to the girl. Her voice trembled with emotion as she spoke. "I can't imagine what it must be like to live in your dark world. I can tell you that I know how it feels to lose both parents. After the explosion, I searched for mine. I am sad to say that they were never found. I have had to accept that they're gone. It has been extremely difficult. But I want you to know that I am very optimistic about the future. I realize that for all that the explosion has taken from us, it has given back as well."

"I want you to know that you are not alone anymore. Fate has brought us together again, and this is for a reason. Do you understand what I mean when I say that fate has brought us together again?" Aubry asked with tears in her eyes.

"I don't know if I do," Janet replied, just a little unsure.

"Sometimes, no matter what we do, we cannot control what happens. Kind of like the explosion. Do you understand that?" Aubry questioned.

"Yes, I think I do," Janet said with conviction.

"It's difficult for me to explain, but there's a reason I found you again. I think it must be part of a grander plan," Aubry said as she leaned in closer. Something Aubry could not explain came over her, and she kissed Janet on the forehead and threw her arms around her in a loving embrace. Tears rolled down her cheeks, and Janet could feel the moisture on her face.

Janet's heart grew bigger in that moment. It had been the first time since the explosion that she had felt affection from anyone, and it felt good. She heard herself asking in a tiny voice, "Why are you crying Miss MacNicholl?" Aubry smiled. She didn't know how to answer that question.

"Janet, I want you to know that I am so sorry for what happened at Camp Hill Hospital. I know I cannot make it right; I never can. But I have thought about that day every day since. I have wondered about you. I have always wanted to know that you are okay. Now I know that you're not. But I am not leaving you, not ever again. That is unless you want me to," Aubry was shaking.

The words that Janet spoke next took Aubry by surprise. "Why are you sorry?" Janet asked.

"I could not protect you. I was the one person in your life that should have been able to keep you safe and I failed," Aubry said.

There was so much more she wanted to say, but she found herself without the courage to speak what was in her heart. She wanted so badly to tell Janet that not only was she sorry she could not protect her from the explosion but she was sorry she could not shield her from the pain that would follow in losing her eyes. Not only that - she was forever affected in having to restrain her while Dr. Drummond removed her eyes. She wanted to tell Janet that she could not forgive herself for the role she played that day. Instead she asked Janet a simple question. "Can you ever forgive me?"

Janet tilted her head in Aubry's direction and revealed what was in her heart. "Forgive you?" she asked. "For what? For taking me to the hospital and making sure I got the treatment I needed? You do not need forgiveness. I was so frightened, so very frightened after the explosion. When I couldn't see, you guided me. When I felt I could not carry on anymore, you reassured me. You did all you could. Please don't ever blame yourself or think that you need to be forgiven for anything because you don't." Janet lowered her head.

Aubry's heart began to heal in that moment. For all the blame she had felt and the burden she had carried with her, a few simple words that came from a girl who had aged years in a mere few months had erased it all. Well, nearly all of it. Yes, Janet's words could not have been more effective, composed or wise.

"Janet, I want you to know something. When I look at you, I see a beautiful young woman with a bright future ahead of her. I agree with you that there is ugliness in this world, and there is pain and suffering. But I want you to know that you don't have to face this world alone. Do you understand me? I couldn't protect you before. But I want to protect you now. Will you let me do that for you?"

Janet held her arms out to embrace Aubry and once again she felt affection she had not felt in months, and her heart soared. "I will try," Janet said.

To Aubry, this was enough for now. "Let's start by going down the stairs and joining the rest of the children. What do you say? You can sit next to me."

"Alright," Janet said even though she was a little apprehensive. She wanted so much not to be alone anymore. Hand in hand, teacher and student walked together, unsure of where the path they were headed down would take them, only knowing that they were together again.

As September drew to a close, Aubry and the children were developing a relationship that was not unlike the close relationship Aubry had developed with her class at St. Joseph's. The children trusted her and often spoke about their lives. Some of the things the children told her deeply disturbed her because she cared so much. Even Janet had come to open up to her. This pleased Aubry and brought her an immense amount of joy.

Patrick still came to Aubry in her dreams nearly every night. For the most part, she could not recall the dreams. Occasionally, she would wake up with his name on her lips in a desperate sort of way and she could feel that in those dreams they had been intimate. Of course, this made her miss him all the more. But still she was glad for his presence and would not have it any other way. If this was the only way she could still feel connected to him, so be it.

Aubry was troubled about the one lingering message Patrick was still attempting to convey: Make it count. She knew he had taken her to his destination and she understood his meaning, at least in part. But she also came to discover that she was missing something crucial in his message. She was confident that in time she would fulfill his request and *would* make it count. For now, she would have to be patient.

She was extremely grateful Patrick had brought her to the steps of the Brunswick Street Orphanage. Being with the children brought her great joy, love and peace. It lifted her spirits in a way that nothing else could.

CHAPTER NINETEEN

One day early in October, Aubry arrived at work at her usual time, wearing her pale blue dress. She had noted the chill in the air and wished she had worn her winter overcoat. She shivered for nearly the entire carriage ride. Even Billy took notice and had asked Aubry if she would like to wear his overcoat. When she had refused, she could see the disappointment in Billy's eyes. She had noted that Billy was of late always clean- shaven and well-presented. She had wondered if there was a lady in his life, and although they had become close, she dared not ask.

When Aubry entered the kitchen to help serve breakfast, Marguerite was the first to comment. "You don't look so well Aubry. Are you feeling alright?"

"I am fine, thank you. I have caught a chill on the way to work. I am sure it's nothing," Aubry responded.

By the time the children were finished their breakfast, and the dishes were being cleared, Aubry was caught in her third sneezing fit, and her eyes were watering profusely.

"It will do us no good to have the children sick. You don't look so well. Go home and rest and come back when you are feeling better," Marguerite instructed firmly. Of course, she was right, and Aubry knew for the sake of the children that she should leave.

At about midmorning, Billy arrived. He had brought Aubry's winter overcoat and a blanket. He helped her into the carriage and took the time to spread the blanket over her. Aubry smiled at him with deep appreciation. She was glad to have Billy. He had always been there for her. She slept for most of the ride home as Billy stole glances of at her.

He remembered the way Patrick had always called her beautiful. That she is, Billy thought to himself.

Billy pulled up to their house on South Street and helped Aubry up the stairs and into bed. This is where Aubry stayed for the better part of the next two weeks. She would find herself unable to sleep much at night due to fits of coughing. She ran a temperature for four days. She soaked through her blankets numerous times. Her throat closed in, and she was barely able to breathe, and unable to talk.

Billy called for a doctor, twice. Dr. Hope expressed deep concern for Aubry and although he felt she would be fine, he was concerned about her fever. He suggested applying a cool cloth to her forehead, and giving her plenty of liquids, if she could swallow. He instructed Billy to keep a watchful eye on her. If her condition worsened, she should be brought to the hospital.

It was with deep worry that Billy bid the doctor farewell the second time. When the fever finally broke on the fourth day, Billy was extremely relieved. It was only then, and with Lily's urging, that he left Aubry's side to get some sleep.

For the next week, Aubry barely left her bed. She had dark circles under her eyes and making her way to the bathroom and back proved to be exhausting. She found herself light-headed and dizzy. Even though Patrick had come to her every night while she was ill, she had no recollection of it.

When, after two weeks Aubry had made her way into the kitchen for some coffee, Lily and Billy were relieved. Lily prepared a fresh pot of coffee and placed a cup in front of Aubry, who drank in silence. Lily wondered where Aubry was because she certainly was not with them. Even Billy noticed. His curiosity got the better of him and he had to ask: "Is everything alright, do you need anything?" Aubry did not respond for several more minutes.

Billy and Lily exchanged questioning glances and sat patiently, waiting for Aubry to speak. Finally, she broke the silence.

"What day is today?" she asked.

"It's Thursday," Billy responded.

"Ah, yes, Thursday. That's good, very good," Aubry replied, still a great distance away. The silence resumed for another few minutes. This was followed by Aubry's heavy sigh. She was contemplating something; Billy could see it but he wasn't sure what.

"The time has come," Aubry said nervously. "The time has come to settle Patrick's affairs. As I am not sure exactly about his finances, I will need to meet with Patrick's lawyer. Can you arrange that for me today, Billy?"

Billy was searching Aubry's face for answers he could not find. He sat down across from her at the table, and she could not see how nervous he was because he fidgeted with his hands under the table.

"Certainly, I will make the request at once. Would you prefer a meeting here or at his lawyer's office?" Billy inquired.

"Prepare the carriage. I will be going out today. I will be ready in an hour." With that, Aubry made her way up stairs.

In about an hour, Aubry reappeared. She looked simply stunning. She was wearing Billy's favourite black dress. It was the perfect length, ending just above her knees and showed an ample amount of bosom. Although Aubry had lost some weight, she still had the same generous curves Billy had always admired. She wore her hair parted to the left side, and it looked so soft, Billy wanted to reach out and grab a handful to see if it was as soft as it looked. He could almost imagine the feeling of her hair between his fingers. He was consumed by her and scarcely noticed that he was daydreaming.

"Is the carriage ready?" Aubry asked.

Billy was brought back from his daydream at the sound of her musical voice. "It certainly is," he affirmed with a smile.

He helped Aubry into the carriage and pulled away. They headed south, and in 16 minutes, they had arrived at the office of Mr. B. Higgins.

Billy had made this trip enough times to know that Aubry would be a while. Mr. B. Higgins was a talker. He truly was a lawyer's lawyer. Patrick had always spoken fondly of him, and Billy knew that Patrick trusted him. Mr. B. Higgins was privy to most all of Patrick's finances and had been for years.

When Aubry emerged an hour later, Billy was not surprised to see that she was quite happy. Whatever had transpired in the office of Mr. B. Higgins had satisfied her. She was smiling and spoke animatedly about Patrick's lawyer.

Although Billy had never met the man, Aubry described him in great detail. He was in his early 50s, Aubry guessed. He was short, stocky and bald. Aubry spoke of how the light shone off his head, and as he moved about his office, pacing between his large oak desk and the framed picture of Sir Robert Borden and himself, the light moved about his head. To Aubry, this was almost as amusing as his thick grey moustache that curled toward his nose. Billy chuckled to himself. Aubry had a way of making him laugh.

After her visit with Patrick's lawyer, Aubry remained tight-lipped about the details. She did dance around the house all weekend, humming incessantly but this did not bother Billy. In fact, he rather enjoyed seeing Aubry this way.

On Monday morning, Aubry returned to her volunteer work, unaware of what had transpired over the last few weeks. Apparently in her absence, the staff had done their best to reassure the children that she would be returning. However, Janet was convinced that Aubry was not coming back. She was so upset that she began to wake in the middle of the night screaming again and had taken to spending her time by herself in her room, only coming downstairs to eat. Marguerite attempted to reassure Janet, but it did nothing to quell the girl's fears.

Aubry found Janet in her room by herself, in the same corner that the girl had been sitting in the first day she had begun teaching life skills to the children. When Aubry entered the room, Janet could smell her right away and straightened up. Aubry went to the girl and slid down the wall to sit next to her.

Janet spoke first. "I thought you weren't coming back," she said.

"I am so sorry you thought that. I have been ill these past few weeks." Aubry leaned in closer and was about to give her a hug. Janet pushed her away.

"You have no idea what it feels like to be me. It's so lonely. No one here talks to me. Sometimes, I think they're afraid of me, like I'm some kind of monster. When you didn't come back, I thought you were afraid too, and I thought it must be true, I must be a monster." Janet's emotions were overwhelming her.

"Oh Janet, I had no idea you felt that way. You are not a monster. I meant what I said. You are beautiful, on the inside and out. I am here with you now and I'm not going anywhere. I won't leave you again, I promise." Aubry threw her arms around Janet and despite the girl's protests, held her tightly. Tears sprang from Aubry's eyes, and her shoulders heaved as she cried. "I won't leave you again," she repeated through quiet sobs, and Janet believed her.

CHAPTER TWENTY

The next several weeks passed by in a haze of excitement and planning. While awaiting word from Mr. B. Higgins, Aubry got to work. Her parents' house needed a great deal of work. She went through the place with a notepad and made a list. She gave the list to Billy and instructed him to hire some help. The entire house needed to be painted inside and out, the floors needed to be washed, the grass needed to be cut and the window in the back needed to be replaced.

Each day for nearly two weeks, Aubry would stop by on her way to work to see the progress. On the last day she stopped in, she could not help but smile. She thought the red she had chosen for the exterior of the house gave it life and charm. The orange shutters were a nice touch too, she thought. It made the house look quite cheerful. A final walk-through revealed a house painted a neutral beige throughout, and a cleanliness that made her inhale very deeply. Aubry was quite pleased.

On the first Sunday in November, Aubry was sitting at the kitchen table sipping coffee. She had slept in and had just now come down for the day. It was already midmorning, and Aubry was only on her first cup. Patrick had come to her last night, and although they were not intimate, they had been kissing and touching one another. She had awakened with his name on her lips. She was daydreaming again and so she did not hear the knock at the door.

Several seconds later, Lily was in the kitchen announcing the presence of Mr. B. Higgins. By the time Lily had uttered his name, Aubry had already rushed past her and was greeting the lawyer inside the front door.

"Good morning, Aubry," Mr. B. Higgins greeted her warmly. "Sorry to interrupt your Sunday. I wanted to tell you just as soon as I could that your late husband's affairs have been settled," the lawyer said with a smile. The words late husband were like a slap in the face, but Aubry let it go. She knew she would hear her husband referred to in ways such as that and she could not let it bother her. People would not understand that Patrick was still very much a part of her life.

"Walk with me," Mr. B. Higgins told Aubry. She grabbed her overcoat and hat and followed him. Aubry could smell and feel the autumn air. It was fresh and cool. The city was colourful this time of year. It really was breathtaking to see the orange, red and yellow leaves, which had fallen off the trees and landed in random patterns. The colours quite reminded Aubry of the stained glass window in her great-uncle's house.

The two walked down South Street and onto Longard Street in silence. As they turned left onto Inglis Street, Aubry began to get anxious and cleared her throat. Sensing what Aubry was just about to ask, Mr. B. Higgins spoke.

"Point Pleasant Park is so lovely this time of year. Nearly every Sunday, I watch the sun rise from the shoreline at the park. Let us walk there, and then I will tell you about Mr. Putnam's affairs." Aubry wondered if Mr. B. Higgins had picked up on her negative feelings toward Patrick being described as her late husband.

It wasn't long before they had reached the park and had walked the trail down the hilly slope to the shoreline. Indeed, the park was inspiring this time of year. Mr. B. Higgins stopped and looked out upon the water. The midmorning sun shone off the water and cast a bright glow in his direction.

It was his turn to clear his throat. "Aubry, I am sure you know Patrick was a wealthy man," he began. Aubry's heart skipped a beat and then beat twice, very fast. This was the moment when her future would be defined, and she would know where to begin. Her biggest questions were about to be answered. She and Patrick had not talked about money. They had never discussed how profitable his businesses were; they had never discussed the future. All Patrick had wanted Aubry to know was that she would be provided for and taken care of. She had not pressed Patrick for any of the details; she simply trusted in him. Now the moment of truth had arrived, and Aubry sighed deeply and stuffed her hands into the pockets of her overcoat. She looked out upon the water and noted how peaceful it looked.

Mr. B. Higgins turned to face Aubry and their eyes met. "Mr. Putnam's accounts have been paid in full. As you know, he was quite a wealthy man. After settling his affairs with his creditors and suppliers, he has left you with a substantial estate. Surely you could rebuild, if you wanted to. Certainly with about $300,000, your future is secure."

Aubry choked back her tears. This was more than she could have hoped for and more than she had planned for. Mr. B. Higgins attempted to read Aubry's expression and he surmised that the widow was more than pleased.

"This is wonderful news, Mr. B. Higgins. I can't thank you enough for your services. But there is something else I require of you," Aubry said, betraying the relief and joy she felt. As she filled the lawyer in on the details, he readily agreed. The two walked out of Point Pleasant Park and parted ways. Aubry took no notice of the autumn chill in the air as she made her way home.

On Tuesday, Aubry was awake before the sun had come up. She was bathed, dressed and ready for the waiting carriage, at just after 7 o'clock in the morning. She was beaming, and Billy's heart fluttered. She looked especially beautiful on this cool and bright morning. Her hair fell loosely in dramatic curls to the right. Billy helped Aubry into the carriage and he guided the horses to the office of Mr. B. Higgins. As the lawyer made his way into the carriage, Aubry looked for reassurance. "Do you have the papers?" she inquired nervously.

"Indeed, everything is in order," Mr. B. Higgins replied, patting his brown leather briefcase.

"Excellent," Aubry exclaimed.

A little before 8 o'clock, the carriage pulled up in front of the Brunswick Street Orphanage. Billy dismounted in time to help Aubry down. Although Mr. B. Higgins was more than capable, Billy never missed his chance to hold Aubry's hand, even if it was only for a few seconds. He cherished her touch. She was still beaming, and this excited Billy. As he made his way back to the driver's seat, he could scarcely stand the anticipation.

Aubry knocked on the door and waited with her lawyer by her side. She was excited and nervous, and a high-pitched laugh escaped her. She was shaking as she fought to keep her emotions under control. Marguerite opened the door and saw Aubry first.

"You're early for work today." Just as Marguerite spoke, she saw the gentleman standing behind Aubry. She observed the look on Aubry's face and said, "Do come in," which sounded more like a question than a statement. She turned her back on them and headed to her office.

Aubry led the way, followed by her lawyer. Once inside Marguerite's office, Aubry shut the door. Marguerite sat down at her desk and gestured to Aubry to sit as well. Aubry took the seat opposite Marguerite. Mr. B. Higgins stood to her right.

Aubry spoke first, "Marguerite, I would like to introduce you to Mr. B. Higgins." In the process of retrieving the file from his brown leather briefcase, the lawyer stopped and extended his hand to Marguerite.

"Pleased to meet you, Marguerite," he said, shaking her hand.

"This is my lawyer," Aubry announced, as Mr. B. Higgins retrieved the file and placed it in front of Marguerite. With a quizzical look, Marguerite started to open the file. But before she had a chance to, Mr.

B. Higgins placed his hand on hers. She was embarrassed when the stranger touched her, and her heart raced. She glanced at Aubry, her expression pleading with her to explain.

Mr. B. Higgins spoke. "Allow me to explain the contents of that file. In that file, you will see that all the papers are in order. All that is missing are the signatures to make it official, the adoption of Janet Moore by Aubry Putnam."

Their eyes locked for a few moments, and then Marguerite looked down at the file in front of her. She opened the file and examined the contents.

"Please go ahead and look through the paperwork. You will see that everything is there," Mr. B. Higgins urged.

Marguerite looked at Aubry, her mouth agape. She could not have foreseen this. Aubry held her breath as Marguerite flipped through the paperwork. As Marguerite examined the last page, she put her hands to her heart and spoke. "This is magnificent. Janet will be so pleased. You are doing a wonderful thing for this child, Aubry," Marguerite said.

No, Aubry thought, this is magnificent. I am so pleased. Janet has done a wonderful thing for me.

Marguerite signed the documents and returned them to the envelope. She rose out of her seat, the chair scrapping against the wooden floor and nearly toppling over. "I will go get her at once. We can tell her together."

Aubry stood up, cutting off Marguerite's path to the door. "Wait, there's more," she said. Marguerite stopped and looked at Aubry curiously. "Please. Sit," Aubry requested.

Marguerite sat back down in her chair. Mr. B. Higgins retrieved another file from his brown leather briefcase and slid it across the desk in front of Marguerite. She opened it and examined the legal document. It was the deed to the land at 138 South Street. Marguerite was shocked as she read the deed over again.

"Please see fit to do as you please with the property at 138 South Street," said Aubry. "The home here has little room, and the children could benefit from the space a second home would provide. It has been prepared and is ready for use today. Or you may choose to sell the property. It brings me great joy to present this to you." She swallowed repeatedly as she fought back tears.

Marguerite allowed *her* tears to flow. "Aubry, this is overwhelming. This means so much to me, and to the children. Your generosity cannot be measured." She wiped her eyes and offered Aubry the most sincere of smiles. For a moment, there was silence. Again Marguerite attempted to rise from her seat. Mr. B. Higgins placed a hand on her left shoulder, which made Marguerite blush again as she took her seat.

Aubry looked at Marguerite for a moment more and then spoke. "There is one more matter to discuss," she said as she gestured towards

Mr. B. Higgins. He reached into his brown leather briefcase and retrieved a third envelope. This he handed to Aubry. She reached inside and pulled out the final piece to her plan.

"On behalf of the estate of Patrick Putnam, I would like to present you with this." Aubry held out a cheque. Marguerite took it from Aubry and almost fainted.

"Aubry, you have done so much already. We cannot accept this," Marguerite's voice was so filled with emotion her words were barely audible.

"You will accept the cheque. Consider it a small token of my appreciation. I have learned a great deal in my time here and I am thankful to be a part of such a wonderful family."

With that statement, Aubry rose and made her way toward the door. Marguerite looked down at the cheque again and blinked. To her amazement, the numbers did not change. With $100,000, Marguerite knew, for the first time in her nearly 15 years of being director, that the children would be okay. In fact, they would be more than okay.

As if walking on air, Marguerite floated into the hallway, the smile never leaving her face, or her heart. Her spirits were lifted in a way that they had never been before. She said goodbye to Mr. B. Higgins, with the hope that she would see him again someday, and she turned to Aubry.

Their eyes met, and neither woman spoke for a minute. Marguerite was seeing in Aubry's eyes, a peace she had never seen before. Aubry broke the silence.

"If it's fine by you, I have arrangements to make. I will return later today for Janet. Also, I would like to tell her myself."

"Yes, that is a wonderful idea," replied Marguerite, who was still very much in awe of what had transpired and was at that moment unable to display any emotion.

"Very well, I will return just as soon as the arrangements are complete," Aubry said excitedly. She smiled at Marguerite and turned away. Outside, Billy and Mr. B. Higgins were waiting for Aubry. The smile on Aubry's face could not be erased as the carriage made its way through the streets of Halifax.

CHAPTER TWENTY-ONE

After taking Mr. B. Higgins back to his law office, the carriage continued on its way to 16 Inglis Street. Billy dismounted from the driver's seat and as always, helped Aubry down from the carriage.

"Thank you, Billy," Aubry said with the same radiant smile she had been wearing since her meeting with Marguerite and her lawyer.

"If I may speak freely, Aubry, it is a wonderful thing that you are doing for Janet." Billy smiled and his eyes met Aubry's.

"It is a tremendous thing that Janet has done for me," Aubry responded. The two made their way into their new home at 16 Inglis Street. Lily was waiting for them.

"Aubry, come with me. I want you to see Janet's room." Lily spoke with more animation than Aubry had ever heard before. In this moment, she looked 10 years younger, and Aubry was almost certain Lily's face had fewer lines, wrinkles and creases.

She followed Lily up the stairs, with Billy close behind. As they entered Janet's room, which was the first room on the right, Aubry beamed. It was perfect. The walls had been painted a light pink. The bed was made up in fresh linens, with a pink bedspread which was darker than the walls. The white lace bed skirt added a feminine touch that was quite pretty. The curtains were also made of frilly white lace. A bookshelf, which was anchored about half way up the wall, ran the length of all four walls. There were no books on it yet. They would be filled in time, Aubry thought, and her heart skipped a beat.

A vision suddenly came to Aubry in which she was reading a book to Janet, who seemed completely enthralled. Indeed she was a captive audience. Another vision came to Aubry in which Janet was reading a

Braille book. Aubry turned to Lily and Billy, who were standing silently behind her, waiting for her to speak.

"This is perfect, don't you agree?" Aubry asked. Billy nodded. Lily smiled and began to hum a song Aubry did not recognize.

"Let us go to the shops now," Aubry squealed with delight. She would buy everything a girl of 12 could ever want or need. She would buy a wardrobe of shoes, dresses, mittens and scarves. She would buy a coat and boots and whatever else she could find.

Several hours later, the carriage, now filled with bags, came to a stop outside the Brunswick Street Orphanage. Aubry instructed Lily to stay with Billy and made her way inside alone. She was nervous and did not know how Janet would react.

Marguerite greeted Aubry in the hallway. "Janet is in her room," she informed Aubry with a smile. "Before you go to her, I wanted to thank you again for everything, Aubry. I cannot begin to express what your generosity means for the children." Marguerite's voice began to tremble and she let her tears of joy rain down in a way that only a spirit that is full and free will allow.

Aubry smiled and embraced Marguerite. "Working here has been an experience like no other. It has changed me in ways that I am sure need no explanation. I am the one who is thankful. I am thankful for the opportunity you have given me to be a part of something greater. You know the children give back in ways that only children can. They are great teachers and their honesty is pure." Aubry let Marguerite go.

It was Aubry's turn to speak with a trembling voice. "Now if I may, I want to bring my daughter home." She was even more nervous and excited. But beyond that, she was scared at hearing herself speak the words, my daughter. The reality started to sink in, and Aubry flushed with anticipation.

She found Janet sitting in the same corner she always sat in. Janet could immediately feel her presence and sat up. Aubry slid down the wall and sat next to Janet, as she always had. It occurred to her that this would be the last time the two of them would sit in this very spot. Aubry's heart searched for the right words, a way to begin.

"Janet, do you remember when I said that you don't have to face this world alone?" Aubry looked to Janet for reassurance. Janet nodded her head. "Do you remember how I said that I wanted to protect you now?" Aubry questioned.

"Yes," she replied, unsure of why Aubry was asking her these questions. Aubry reached out and took the girl's hand in hers. Janet could feel that Aubry's hand was moist.

"Do you remember when I said that I am not going anywhere and that I won't leave you again?" Without waiting for an answer, Aubry continued. "I have found a way for us to be together, to be a family. I will provide for you and protect you. You're coming home with me to live, forever." Aubry threw her arms around Janet and felt an all-consuming joy.

Her joy was short-lived as Aubry could feel Janet's body become rigid. "Do you understand Janet? I have made the arrangements to adopt you. We're a family now," Aubry reassured her. Still Janet did not relax.

"What's wrong, Janet? I thought you would be happy. Say something," Aubry urged. She was nearly panicking. This was not how she had envisioned the conversation unfolding. She thought Janet would be ecstatic. She let the girl go and looked down at her.

"Miss MacNicholl, I really do appreciate the gesture. But if it's okay by you, I will stay here."

Aubry was stunned. She was heartbroken. She asked the only question that needed to be asked. "Why?" Her upper lip was quivering and she could feel that the tears welling up were on the verge of breaking free.

"Listen," Janet began, "I know you must have gone to a lot of trouble and I am grateful. But when you said that you have found a way for us to be together, to be a family, that's when I knew that my place would always be right here." Janet looked very troubled as the lines on her forehead deepened.

"I don't understand," Aubry began. "You don't want a life with me? You don't want to be a family? Why?" Her mind was racing. She couldn't keep up with the questions that were being posed internally.

It was Janet's turn to ask a question. "How do you define a family?" But before Aubry could formulate an answer to a question she hadn't anticipated being asked, Janet ploughed on. "Again, it's really swell that you thought we could be a family, but in my definition of a family, one word comes to mind, love."

"I do love you, Janet. I love you in a way that is unconditional, a way that a mother ought to love a daughter. And I always will." Tears ran down Aubry's face. She was caught in a moment that would be life-changing. It was a moment where what came next would define who she was and what her future would be. All at once, she understood Janet's trepidation and hesitation.

"You love me?" Janet asked.

"Yes, I do love you, Janet."

Janet reached up and touched Aubry's face. When she withdrew her hand, her finger was wet. "I love you too." Janet spoke these four words, and Aubry threw her arms around Janet in a moment that was etched in her heart forever. The two of them were silent for a few minutes and held on to each other tight.

Janet drew in a breath and spoke. "I will come with you now."

Aubry kissed Janet's forehead, and tears of joy burst forth. Her shoulders shook and she laughed nervously. "Gather your belongings. Let us go home."

Janet started claiming all that was hers.

About 20 minutes later, two figures emerged from the oprhanage. Hand in hand, they made their way to the carriage. Billy leapt down from the carriage to help Janet and Aubry. Marguerite followed closely behind with Janet's bags.

"Janet, I would like to introduce you to Lily and Billy," Aubry said.

Janet smiled and waved her hand. "Hi," she said shyly.

Aubry explained that Lily and Billy were also part of the family and that they would live with them too and help with the running of the house day to day.

"Oh," Janet replied with a giggle, "We have housekeepers."

"Yes, something like that," Aubry said.

"It is nice to meet you, Janet," said Lily.

Billy chuckled to himself. He found Janet's reaction quite amusing. "Hello Miss Janet," he said in a voice that seemed to express that he was speaking to someone of high importance. This made Janet giggle again. Aubry flashed Billy a smile that seemed to express gratitude for making the moment light. Somehow Billy always seemed to know what was required of him.

The carriage pulled up to their new home. Billy vacated the driver's seat and helped Aubry, Janet and Lily down. He then retrieved all of the bags and followed awkwardly behind. As Lily opened the door, Aubry led Janet inside. Janet inhaled the scent of her new home for the first time. It was pleasant, slightly sweet and clean. It smelled much better than her room at the orphanage.

Aubry led Janet up to her room, and Janet was even more pleased with how her room smelled. It was not that her room at the orphanage smelled horrible; it was just that it held within its walls the scent of other children. But this house smelled of Aubry, which she liked, and this room did not smell of other children. Before long, it would only smell of one child, her. Janet liked that very much and smiled.

She carefully walked to her bed and sat down. The bed was soft, and the sheets were fresh, and she liked the feel of the comforter. She knew she would sleep soundly. Janet asked Aubry to describe her room, which she did in great detail. Janet was pleased to hear that her room was pink, as well as her bedding.

Next, Aubry presented Janet with her new clothes, and Janet beamed. One by one, Aubry took the clothing out of the bags and Janet examined each garment individually as Aubry described each one. She was especially impressed with her new overcoat, which was pink, double-breasted and flared out at the bottom. When she tried it on, it fell past her knees and she knew it would keep her warm in the winter.

CHAPTER TWENTY-TWO

Christmas neared, and Aubry and Janet settled into a routine that was orderly and happy. Aubry still volunteered at the Brunswick Street Orphanage, and Janet attended the Halifax School for the Blind. After classes let out, Billy would pick up Janet and most days, he would take her to the Brunswick Street Orphanage. Then at 5 o'clock, Billy would pick them up and take them home.

In the evenings, Billy escorted Aubry as she shopped for Christmas gifts. Lily stayed behind with Janet. The girl would often entertain Lily with stories of her school day, and sometimes Lily would read to her. Janet was developing a keen interest in literature and enjoyed writers such as Jane Austen, Charles Dickens and Edgar Allen Poe.

Two days before Christmas, Janet awoke to the smell of Lily's baking. She remembered when her mother used to bake for Christmas, usually each day for about a week. Janet's heart pained her so at the memory of her mother and father. Aubry was giving her a wonderful life. But it seemed the closer she and Aubry became, the more her heart ached for her mother and father. She did not understand why, it just did. She could not bring herself to talk to Aubry about her feelings, so she did her best to keep her sadness to herself and keep on smiling.

Janet made her way carefully down the stairs and into the kitchen.

"I trust you like gingerbread." Lily stated this more as a fact than a question.

"Very much so," Janet affirmed.

"Ah, you won't mind having some for breakfast, then." Again Lily put this as more of a fact than a question. She offered a cookie to Janet, and the girl hungrily accepted. It tasted so good, just like the ginger-bread her mother used to make. Lily observed the expression on Janet's face change. She could tell some feeling had just washed over the girl, and she was concerned.

After pressing Janet a bit, Lily found the girl opening up to her. Janet expressed her sadness over her parents, and Lily understood that she was still in mourning. Janet begged her not to say anything to Aubry. She reassured Janet that she would not. This would be the first among many conversations that would strengthen the bond between Lily and Janet, something they both needed.

Shortly after breakfast, Billy arrived with excitement in his voice and a Christmas tree in tow. He struggled through the house with it, leaving a trail of needles. With Lily's help, he erected the tree in the front sitting room. Janet allowed the scent of the forest to fill her. For the first time in a very long time, she was excited about something.

Janet remembered that her first Christmas after the explosion had been miserable. She was at the orphanage, recovering from the loss of her eyes. Her world was very dark, so much so that her nightmares were her escape. In her nightmares, she could see again. So for her, it was quite emotional. She would still wake up terrified and screaming and yet she was thankful to have seen, if only for a little while.

Lily, Janet and Billy sang Christmas carols as they decorated the tree. Aubry entered the room just as the three had sung the last few words of Jingle Bells. Aubry thought they sounded wonderful and clapped her hands in delight. The three turned toward Aubry, surprised at her presence.

Billy's heart beat harder as he smiled at Aubry. She seemed not to notice as her attention was focused on Janet. It had been a long time since she had seen Janet so happy. Aubry was overjoyed and she ran to Janet, took her in her arms and danced her around the room.

When she stopped, she was laughing and trying to catch her breath. Janet was laughing too, and they collapsed under the tree in a heap. Billy never took his eyes away from Aubry and even from across the room he was intoxicated by her smell. Lily shot Billy a look of disapproval, of which he took no notice.

"The tree looks beautiful," Aubry said from underneath. She turned to Janet, who was lying next to her. "It has the most wonderful red garland, and there are ornaments of green, silver, red and gold. It's so pretty. This is going to be a wonderful Christmas, don't you think, Janet? After all, we're together." Aubry playfully ran her fingers through Janet's hair.

Janet smiled. She certainly was happy to be spending Christmas with Aubry, Billy and especially Lily. "Yes, I do think this Christmas will be wonderful," Janet agreed.

Christmas Eve brought a light dusting of snow to Halifax, which made the port city look picturesque. Aubry, Janet, Lily and Billy had just returned from St. Mary's Church on Spring Garden Road. Father John

Forrester had delivered a solemn homily, in which he spoke of rebirth, love and forgiveness. Sister Mary had observed Aubry arrive hand in hand with Janet. She had heard of Aubry's generous donation and had been even more pleased upon hearing the news of the adoption. When she saw Aubry and Janet leave together, she knew she was witnessing something greater than religion and she nodded in approval.

At home, Janet prepared for bed. She was eager for the arrival of morning.

Aubry drew the blankets over Janet and kissed her on her cheek. "Good night, beautiful," she whispered as she blew the candle out.

"Good night to you, too," Janet whispered in response. As Aubry turned and left, Janet was unsure if Aubry had heard her.

As the sun rose in the sky over Halifax, Janet heard the muffled voices of Aubry, Lily and Billy coming from the kitchen. She smelled the familiar aroma of coffee and knew it was time. Janet suddenly appeared before them in the kitchen. Aubry was quite surprised, as it was routine for her to help Janet down the stairs, and this was the first time she had seen Janet take the stairs by herself. Aubry was quite pleased to see that Janet was becoming more independent.

"Good morning," Janet greeted all of them.

"Merry Christmas, Janet," Aubry said, giving her a hug.

"Can I have breakfast after we open presents?" Janet asked.

"Of course," Aubry said with a giggle.

They made their way into the front sitting room. Presents covered the floor under the tree. There was scarcely room to sit. Yet, somehow Aubry and Janet found room. As Lily and Billy observed from a distance, Aubry passed Janet her gifts. Janet delighted in receiving books, as she was in the midst of learning Braille. She also received clothes, dolls and records.

Aubry had saved the best gift for last. She handed the small present to Janet. When Janet took the present in her hands, she was surprised at how heavy it was. She peeled back the brown paper the gift was wrapped in and could immediately smell that it was made of pewter. She ran her fingers over the raised edges and could feel the design of a hummingbird. She lifted the lid and the material inside was velvety to the touch. Janet liked the way it felt under her fingertips.

"It's a jewelry box," Aubry proclaimed. "Do you like it?'

"It's perfect, Janet reassured her, although she was a little puzzled with the gift as she owned no jewelry.

"There is one more gift I have for you, "Aubry said as she reached her hand out to take the box Billy gave her.

She handed the box to Janet. It was small and light. Janet carefully took off the paper it was wrapped in. A delicate gold bracelet dangled from her fingers. Janet explored the smooth piece of jewelry with her fingers.

Aubry spoke. "I made a promise that we will always be together. When I am not with you, I want you to think of my promise, and when you feel the bracelet as it moves back and forth against your skin, I want you to remember that I am with you. Let me put it on for you."

Aubry took the bracelet from Janet and opened the clasp. Janet held out her left wrist, and Aubry secured the clasp once again.

"Thank you so much," Janet said with a smile in her voice. She reached out for Aubry, and their embrace lingered. When Janet moved away, she felt her bracelet move back and forth against her skin and each time it did, just as Aubry said, she was reminded of Aubry and reminded of how it felt to feel love again. Janet began to heal a little more with each passing day.

CHAPTER TWENTY-THREE

Aubry healed a little more with each passing day as well. Patrick was still very much a part of this healing process. He still came to her in her dreams, and oftentimes, Aubry still awoke with his name on her lips. One such morning, in early April, Aubry opened her eyes to the sound of birds chirping outside her window. She had dreamed of Patrick the night before. Now she heard his voice calling for her, with the resounding message, "Come to me."

She knew what she had to do. She had put if off for as long as she could, but she could put it off no longer. Patrick was urging her now and he would not be denied.

She knew she had to go to Patrick that very day. She just had to gather her courage and prepare herself. She did her best to delay his request. But at last, she knew the time had come. She instructed Billy to prepare the carriage. She emerged from the house wearing a modest and simple black dress, which she kept hidden under her overcoat. The day was still not without a chill in the air.

Billy helped Aubry into the carriage.

"Take me to Patrick, please. I need to see where he is buried." Aubry's command was firm, and it took Billy by surprise. He was at a loss for words as he took his place in the driver's seat.

He drove the carriage thought the streets of Halifax and towards Mount Olivet Cemetery. When the carriage came to a stop, Billy stepped down from the carriage and reached for Aubry's hand to help her down. Their eyes met, and Billy shivered. He saw in Aubry's eyes a coolness he could not recall seeing before. She seemed flat and vacant, and this terrified him.

"Wait here," Aubry said coldly. Billy fumbled in his pockets and shuffled his feet. He watched Aubry as she made her way deeper into the cemetery and fade from his view. He leaned up against the carriage and regarded the late-day sun.

Aubry wandered about the cemetery in search of Patrick. It was not unlike her search after the explosion in that it was exhaustive and taxing on her soul. When at last she found his grave marker, she collapsed in front of it. She ran her slender fingers over his name, carefully feeling each letter that was imperfectly etched in the granite. An "Oh," escaped her lips as she looked upon the name of the only man she had ever truly loved.

Aubry could feel Patrick's presence, and it was powerful. It illuminated her soul, warmed her heart and coursed through her veins, invading her entire body. She was instantly more alert, more aware and more alive. Memories of Patrick's touch caused her to shiver. She let out a heavy sigh that she did not notice. She ran her fingers through her hair, her eyes never leaving his name.

"Here I am," she spoke out loud. "I have come to you as you have compelled me to do. Surely you can understand why it took me so long." Aubry paused and drew a breath.

"I am making it count, Patrick. I know it's what you want. I know that's why I am still here. There's still so much more for me to do, so much more for me to accomplish. And I will continue to do the work you cannot. So long as I have your guidance, for as long as you're with me, I will continue to live my life for you." Aubry tensed for a moment, although she was unsure why.

"Without you, without your guidance, I make terrible choices. We both know that," Aubry continued. For a moment, her soul was blackened as she recalled her time with Judas. The memory of his face made her recoil. Her infidelity and subsequent pregnancy made her cringe. "Without you, Patrick, I am nothing. I am not worthy of anything, not even the air I breathe," Aubry admitted.

"But with you, with your guidance, I have purpose, and the air I breathe is not wasted. I am worthy. You are my strength and my courage. You are a good man. You have brought me out of my darkest days, when I was on the edge of destruction and I was lost. You have been my reason to carry on and my reason to believe in a better tomorrow." Aubry closed her eyes and fell silent. She allowed herself to be in the moment. A cool breeze played with her hair and then was gone. She felt the sun warm her face once again. She sat there for quite some time.

Her body tingled, and she opened her eyes. She was excited about the future, about tomorrow and each day thereafter.

"It's almost time for me to go, I can feel it." She knew there wasn't much more to be said. "I will always love you, Patrick. For as long as you are with me, I know I will be okay. My life will have purpose and meaning. I look forward to our future together and what more you have to reveal to me."

Aubry ran her slender fingers over his name once more. A great and powerful energy surged through her body, and the most amazing light blinded her. She could feel the same tingling as she had felt before, and it rushed through her and passed through her fingertips. Her body hitched forward as the energy and heat left her. She closed her eyes just as the blinding light disappeared. The granite grave marker was hot to the touch, and Aubry pulled her fingertips away and opened her eyes.

Peace washed over her, and she rose to her feet. She heard a crow in the distance. She could almost convince herself that it was trying to convey something of vital importance to her as it cawed wildly and flew overhead.

Aubry turned her back on Patrick's grave marker and slowly walked away. She felt lighter somehow. With each step, she grew more confident that her future held the promise that each day would be a blessing and that each day would be better than the one before.

Aubry meandered through the graveyard with a lighter spirit. She was ready to face the future. She was strong enough now to speak of the day when Judas had taken all that mattered in this world from her. She was courageous enough to recount the events to the police and she would tend to this matter in due time.

Her smile grew bigger as she approached Billy. At the sight of Billy, Aubry's heart beat just a little faster, and she took notice. She was thankful for Billy and for a brief second, she wondered why her heartbeat had just quickened. But she was unaware of the feelings she was developing for Billy, and so for the moment, they went undefined.

She did not notice that she was being watched and being followed. She was oblivious to the fact that in the shadows, a figure stood secretly contemplating her future as well.

As she made her way towards a waiting Billy, who still hadn't noticed her approaching, she could not have known that her future would be drastically different than she had envisioned. She could not know that her heart would break time and again and that she was destined to a life that was dark and miserable and without love.

She certainly could not know that Patrick would never again come to her in her dreams. She could not have realized that he had left her as she withdrew her fingertips from his grave marker and that she would once again find herself in a dark place.

She also could not have known that she had not fulfilled Patrick's request to make it count. In failing to understand his meaning and carry out his request before he left her, she could not have known that she had not only failed herself, but also all those closest to her, including Janet. And she could not have known that it was all about to unfold before her very eyes, leaving her alone and in a darker place than she had ever been.

As she made her way towards Billy, she was being watched. Billy, with his back to her heard her approach. He looked down at his hands, at what he was contemplating. He turned the gold locket over and saw for the thousandth time the inscription 01/02/1917 AM. He turned it back over. He knew it would bring Aubry great joy to have her locket back and he couldn't wait to give it to her.

Billy had found the locket under Aubry's bed in the days after Patrick's murder. He had waited for the right time to give it to her and had hesitated until today. Aubry had refused to truly start her grieving process, and he was convinced that until she did, she was not strong enough. Until she did, giving it back to her would only upset her. Now though, he thought the time was right.

"Billy," Aubry called. At the sound of her voice, something Billy could not explain came over him. Without thinking, he stuffed the locket back into his pocket and turned to face the only woman he had ever truly loved. Their eyes met and he searched hers in an attempt to understand what she was thinking.

"Billy," Aubry said again, moving in closer to him. She smiled up at him, and he understood that there was something different about her. He understood that for the first time ever, Aubry was looking at him and seeing him for the man he was, and not her employee. He thought that maybe, just maybe, they could forget all else, forget about the past and look toward their future. He thought that maybe, just maybe, she could love him.

He fumbled in his pocket and felt for the locket. He found it and turned it over in his hand. He would get rid of it once and for all, the first opportunity he had. He withdrew his hand and looked deeper into Aubry's eyes. He tried in vain to look deep into her soul.

It did not matter, though, and he knew it. For whatever this moment was, he would take it. He realized that she was looking at him in a way that she never had before. He fooled himself into thinking that there was a kindness in her eyes that he had never seen before. And he convinced himself that Aubry was ready for the next step.

He could have kissed her in that moment in the cemetery, with the late-day sun warming their faces and their future ahead of them. He imagined leaning in closer for a taste of her sweet lips. And although he could have kissed her in that moment, he did not. There would be a time and place for that later, he thought, and he would know that time and place, which he understood was not now.

Instead, in a bold move he put his arms around her. It was an awkward embrace at first, which she allowed. In a few moments, they relaxed and it felt natural, it felt right. They walked towards the carriage, Billy's arm around Aubry. They were silent, each consumed with their own thoughts, and each looking forward to a future they would never have.

As the sun set over Halifax, Aubry and Billy made their way to the waiting carriage. The shadowy figure's eyes never left the couple as he balled his aged and murderous hand into a tight fist and raised it towards the crimson sky, shaking it madly. A crow flew overhead, and its cry pierced the twilight, drowning out the sinister promise of tomorrow and the evil cackle that followed.

CPSIA information can be obtained at www.ICGtesting.com
Printed in the USA
LVOW040807210912

299654LV00001B/27/P

9 781460 200063